Also in Pyramid Books
by
BARBARA CARTLAND

LOVE IS
DANGEROUS

Barbara Cartland

▲ PYRAMID BOOKS • NEW YORK

LOVE IS DANGEROUS

A PYRAMID BOOK

Pyramid edition published January 1972
 Third printing, August 1972

© Barbara McCorquodale 1963
© Barbara Cartland 1969

All Rights Reserved

ISBN 0-515-02611-5

Printed in the United States of America

Pyramid Books are published by Pyramid Communications, Inc.
Its trademarks, consisting of the word "Pyramid" and the por-
trayal of a pyramid, are registered in the United States Patent
Office.

Pyramid Communications, Inc., 919 Third Avenue,
New York, N.Y. 10022

1

"You are both incompetent and impudent!"

Mrs. Schuster rose as she spoke and crossed the room to the writing-desk by the window.

"Here is a week's wages and your hotel room is paid for the next two days."

Melina could not help thinking that Mrs. Schuster was giving a fine theatrical performance. This was not the spontaneous impulse of the moment but a carefully thought-out, preconceived action. Then as she took the envelope automatically and felt it heavy with coins to make it exactly the right amount, she knew that whatever she had said or done that particular day the ultimate result would have been the same.

Yet because she was so desperate she had to argue.

"I don't understand," she said. "I'm sorry if you did tell me to be back by two o'clock, but I certainly don't remember your saying so: and as to bringing you a particular book from the English Library, I've never heard you mention it before."

"You don't listen, that is what's wrong with you," Mrs. Schuster retorted. "I did tell you to be back at two and I did ask you to get me Rom Landau's book on Morocco. However, there's no point in going over this again. It's only typical of several incidents in the last fortnight and I'm afraid I cannot put up with it any longer. When I brought you here I was looking for someone who would consider me and my interests."

"Mrs. Schuster, that's not fair!" Melina broke out. "I have considered you in every possible way. You asked me to come with you to Tangier to drive your car and to do any secretarial work that was required."

5

"You can't say there's much of that!" Mrs. Schuster interrupted.

"No, not a lot," Melina admitted. "But there have been other things."

She was thinking—although it was hardly worth saying so—that Mrs. Schuster had used her in a great many capacities besides that of secretary-companion. She had acted as lady's maid for one thing—pressing Mrs. Schuster's clothes, packing and unpacking for her, carrying parcels up and down stairs and doing dozens of small things which should have been done by the hotel servants.

At the same time, Melina knew, everything had been perfectly all right until Ambrose Wheatley arrived. His appearance had been unexpected, but it had been quite obvious that Mrs. Schuster was not only delighted to see him but found that another woman making the party *a trois* was not at all to her liking.

Melina had not been so stupid as not to realise that Lileth Schuster wanted Ambrose to herself, and she had been as self-effacing as possible, making excuses to go out at lunchtime to see the museums and slipping away upstairs as soon as dinner was over so as to leave them alone.

That might have worked if Ambrose Wheatley had not shown her such marked attention.

"Let us drive along by the sea this afternoon," Mrs. Schuster would suggest. "It's a lovely day and I adore the way you drive, Ambrose dear."

"Of course," he would answer. "And what about Melina? She must come too." He would smile at Melina and as he did so she would see Mrs. Schuster's eyes darken.

It was annoying enough for her employer that the young man of her choice should call her secretary by her Christian name while she kept very strictly to the formal, "Miss Lindsay". But that he should wish to include her in the party was intolerable and she let Melina know it in no uncertain manner.

"It's hopeless," Melina thought now, "and there's no point in arguing. The break was inevitable."

With a little gesture of pride she straightened her shoulders.

"Very well, Mrs. Schuster," she said. "I accept a week's notice . . . but . . . but what about my fare back to England?"

"I can't remember that we made any arrangements about that when I engaged you," Mrs. Schuster answered coldly.

Melina was so astonished that she could not speak.

"I am afraid I cannot take any responsibility for you other than to pay you for a week's work you will not do," Mrs. Schuster went on. "Mr. Wheatley and I are leaving tomorrow for Marrakesh and so, Miss Lindsay, I'm afraid you must look after yourself."

So this was her revenge, Melina thought. She knew well enough what it would mean to the girl to be left alone in Tangier without the money to return home. She had thought Lileth Schuster to be pretty unscrupulous on several occasions, but now she knew her to be utterly and completely despicable. It was a shoddy, dirty action and one that only a woman of her calibre would attempt.

"You know as well as I do," she said aloud, "that the arrangement was that I should go with you to Tangier for your holiday and go back with you to England."

"I cannot remember saying anything of the sort," Mrs. Schuster replied. "Just as you, Miss Lindsay, cannot remember my instructions to you to return at two o'clock."

"And what do you suggest I do?" Melina said. "Because, quite frankly, I haven't got my fare back to England."

Mrs. Schuster shrugged her shoulders.

"I believe the British Consulate can provide for British subjects stranded in such a manner," she said. "But anyway, I'm afraid I cannot concern myself with it. Perhaps you can get a job out here. I'm sure some of the rich Moroccans would be only too delighted to employ an attractive English girl!"

There was an unpleasant insinuation in her voice which made Melina long to throw her paltry week's wages at her feet and then march out of the room. But as she realised that such a dramatic gesture would only hurt herself, she merely walked towards the door, pausing as she opened it to say:

"Good-bye, Mrs. Schuster, and thank you for bringing me to Tangier."

She could not help feeling, as her late employer did not reply, that she had scored points in dignity if nothing else, but that in itself was cold comfort as she took the lift to the top floor where her bedroom was situated.

She had not, as they say, "taken to" Mrs. Schuster at their first interview but she had wanted, above all things, to go to Tangier. When she had seen the advertisement in *The Times* asking for a driver-secretary-companion she had made up her mind that whatever the hardships of the journey she would put up with them just for the joy of seeing the country she had always longed to visit.

Then having obtained the job after being interviewed by Mrs. Schuster in her luxurious flat in Grosvenor Square, she had thought herself the luckiest person in the world. It was only after they had crossed the Channel and were motoring through France and then Spain that the first doubts began to creep in.

She had learned in the first twenty-four hours of her acquaintance that Mrs. Schuster was exceedingly mean. She always had the best, naturally; but Melina, as a matter of course, had also to put up with the worst.

She had the worst room looking out on to the little, hot, airless courtyard or over the kitchens of the hotels. She ate with her employer, but while Mrs. Schuster chose caviar, oysters and every possible expensive dish from the menu, Melina ate the *table d'hôte* meal and even then Mrs. Schuster tried to get a cut price on it.

"It's nonsense for people to say that the water in

8

France isn't good," she would say. "The whole idea is fostered by the hoteliers who wish to sell their mineral waters."

It was very likely true, but Melina could not help wondering why her employer did not feel uncomfortable as, having said that once on every day of their journey, she ordered herself wine or half a bottle of champagne and the inevitable demi-Evian.

It was quite obvious from the outset that she had to have her pound of flesh where Melina was concerned.

"It's not worth sending these things to the laundry," she would say, producing an armful of underclothes, blouses, gloves, stockings and handkerchiefs. "Just wash them out, there's a good girl. You can hang them by your window, everything dries so quickly in this wonderful air."

She always spoke of the air and the sunshine as if she had given them as a special present to Melina and expected her to thank her for them.

But Melina had not minded all these things. There was always the excitement of knowing that Morocco lay ahead. She would dream about it at night, making pictures in her mind of what it would be like, remembering all the illustrations she had seen of Tangier, Marrakesh, the Atlas Mountains and the golden shores of Casablanca. They were names to conjure with, names which seemed to her to glitter almost like diamonds every time she thought of them.

And now, after she had been in Tangier only six days, this had happened. She got out of the lift on the fifth floor and walked down the narrow passage to her room.

The room itself was small and unpretentious and yet it had something which meant more to Melina than the luxurious suite on the first floor occupied by Mrs. Schuster. It had a balcony! It was small and square between high walls on either side so that she was secluded from the occupiers of the next rooms, but there was a window-box filled with brightly coloured geraniums and over them Melina could see the flat roofs of

9

Tangier dazzling white against the vivid blue of the sea.

She had never expected to be so fortunate in her accommodation. The receptionist who had taken her up had explained the reason.

"*Madame* has asked for one of our cheap single rooms looking on to the street," he said, "but they are already all engaged. So because *Madame* is such a good client we have put you in this one for the same price. It is a double room really," he said looking at the two small beds squeezed together and occupying most of the space in the room, "but there's a private bathroom."

"Thank you for letting me have it," Melina had smiled. "And thank you, too, for allowing Mrs. Schuster to have it so cheaply."

She was sincere in thanking him for that. She knew by now how Mrs. Schuster would have grumbled and complained about the unnecessary extravagance if they had insisted on charging more for her secretary's bedroom.

How absurd, Melina had thought then, as she had thought so often before, to be so rich and so mean at the same time. Clothes, jewels, furs, motor cars and expensive furniture; all these things were necessities to Lileth Schuster, but everyone else must have as little as possible. Economy on other people was an obsession with her.

Entering her bedroom now, Melina stood for a moment inside the door and looked to where the open window on to the balcony let in a blaze of golden light. The white walls, the geraniums cascading crimson against them and the blue sky above—it was something, she thought, that she would never forget for the rest of her life.

She had been feeling depressed and unhappy. Now her spirits rose. She had seen Tangier! At least she had known for six days the intoxicating excitement of those flat-roofed houses, of the native streets, the veiled, shapeless figures of women, the smell of mimosa and, above all, the inscrutable, mysterious atmosphere of the Middle East. It had invaded her senses, it had quick-

10

ened her heartbeats and had made her feel, as she had known all the time she would feel, that she was on the edge of something important and exciting.

Melina walked across the room and on to the balcony. The sun was suddenly hot on her bare head and turning her hair to a fiery red as she raised her little face towards it. She felt as if the warmth and strength of it kissed her. She felt the comfort and the power of it. Then in a sudden misery she knew that she would have to leave it all behind.

"I can't go! I can't!" she whispered. "I have wanted so much to come here and now to have to leave after seeing so little of Morocco."

At the back of her mind she knew her protests were useless, that she must do as Mrs. Schuster scornfully suggested. She must go to the Consulate, explain her position and ask them to lend her third-class fare home.

She would promise to repay it. She would be able to do that, not in small installments but almost as soon as she got back. There was a brooch of her mother's—a diamond star that she had kept when everything else had to be sold, because she had loved it so much.

She could see it now nestling in her mother's hair as she had come to say good night to her.

"Where are you going, Mummy?"

"To a party with Daddy. Go to sleep like a good girl. I'll tell you all about it tomorrow."

How lovely she had looked! Melina gave a little sigh and opened her eyes. The diamond star would have to go although somehow she felt that she betrayed her mother's memory in getting rid of it. But her father would understand. He would know why she had to see Morocco; why it meant so much.

She bent forward to touch the scarlet geraniums with gentle fingers. She could telegraph to her Uncle and Aunt at Wimbledon, but she knew, if she did, what tiresome explanations there would be when she got back.

Why had she been so stupid as to throw up her good

11

job in that nice solicitor's office? It was so ridiculous to go junketing half across the world and then get stranded so that she had had to ask them for money.

She could hear their voices reiterating the same things over and over again, being annoyed by her behaviour and finally forcing her to admit that the whole adventure had been stupid and misconceived and that she had made a fool of herself.

No, no, she wouldn't eat humble pie to them. They meant well, but they wanted her to be safe and secure and clamped down in that deadly solicitor's office, month after month, year after year, so that they could feel they had done their best for her in getting her the job in the first place.

No! The diamond star would have to go—but at least she had two more days—in Heaven.

She sat down on the tiny wooden seat which was fixed to one of the walls on the balcony. The space was too small for a chair but the hotel had done its best to provide a seat. She raised her face to the sun and let her head drop back against the warm brick wall behind her. She could feel the warmth of it through her thin cotton dress; she felt the sun again on her eyes and on her lips almost like the kiss of a lover.

"I mustn't stay like this for long," Melina thought to herself. "It's too hot. I shall get sunstroke. But it's so wonderful to feel it—the sun of Morocco."

She could smell the sweet fragrance of mimosa drifting up from the gardens. She could hear in the distance the cries from the native market which lay below the hotel on a different level. The voices were like a note of music one has always been trying to hear and could never quite remember until it came again.

"I'm happy," Melina thought suddenly. "Happier than I have ever been in my whole life, despite the fact that I have lost my job and I'm here alone."

Perhaps that was what was making her so happy, she mused—the fact that she was no longer trammelled. She was free; free to do as she wished for two days—or until the money she held in her hand ran out.

12

She realised in surprise that she was still holding it, and laughing a little at herself she bent forward and threw it through the open window on the nearest of the twin beds. The envelope burst open and the money lay there scattered—six pounds, three half-crowns, two shillings and a threepenny-bit. Mrs. Schuster had paid her exactly, Melina noted with a little smile, having deducted her national insurance.

She laughed at the thought. There was something ridiculous, somehow, in Mrs. Schuster with her twenty-thousand-pound diamond ring on her finger and her two-thousand-pound mink stole draped over the chair, deducting the money for national insurance stamps.

"I'm free!"

Melina said the words aloud and this time there was laughter in her voice.

It was then that a sudden noise startled her. There was a scuffle, the sound of a tile falling and smashing; then almost before she could realise what was happening a figure came flying off the roof and on to the balcony beside her.

She stared wide-eyed, too surprised and, a second later, too frightened to move. It was an Arab, his face shadowed by his cotton kosia, but there was a gash of blood on his cheek while his right hand clasped a short, bloodstained knife.

They stared at each other and his dark eyes seemed to Melina to glitter frighteningly. . . . There was a shout from somewhere above! The Arab looked up swiftly, then turned his face towards her again.

"You're English?" he asked, and to her surprise he spoke in English.

Melina nodded; somehow her voice would not come.

"Then help me," he begged. "Help me, because it is of the utmost importance. There is no time to explain, but I am not what I appear. I won't hurt you. The men who are after me are evil and if they catch up with me they will kill me. It sounds rather like something from the movies, but it happens to be true."

There was another cry from above and it seemed to

13

Melina as if it was nearer. The man stepped into her bedroom.

"Where can I hide?" he asked.

With an effort, as if she awoke from same strange, incredible dream, Melina found her voice.

"The . . . the bathroom is the only place."

"Good," he said. "Keep them out as long as you can. Tell them anything—that I'm your husband—but for God's sake give me time."

He crossed the room in one quick stride and she heard the bathroom door slam behind him. She stared, thinking that she must have dreamed it. A native dressed as he was could not have spoken in English which she knew without any shadow of a doubt was his natural tongue. What could it mean? Was it a trick?

She saw her money lying on the bed. Was he after that? And then even as her thoughts rushed bewildered through her head, a tile crashed down on the floor of the balcony and a moment later two men came scrambling after it. They were Moroccans, dressed in native clothes, and she saw with a feeling of sickness that they both carried knives in their hands.

Almost without thinking of what she should do she took the initiative.

"What are you doing here?" she asked. "What do you want?"

Her tone was aggressive and she saw that it seemed to surprise the men who glanced quickly at each other and then back at her. One of them, a tall, dark man with a small moustache, replied in broken English with a pronounced accent:

"The man—he has come down here. . . . We saw him."

There was something about both these Moroccans which made Melina decide that the first man had been right. They were evil and she could not trust them.

"You are mistaken," she said firmly. "It must have been some other balcony. Certainly nobody has come this way."

"We saw him," the man repeated, while the smaller

14

man muttered something in Arabic which obviously confirmed what had been said.

It was then, sliding slowly from the roof behind them, they were joined by a third man. He was fatter and older than the other two and he was out of breath, but Melina saw that he wore the uniform of a police officer.

The taller man who had spoken first quite obviously relayed in Arabic his conversation with Melina and the police officer, still breathless, took the initiative.

"My men tell me that a criminal who has escaped from us dropped on to your balcony, *Madame,*" he said with an air of authority.

"Your men are mistaken," Melina replied. "I was sitting on the balcony a moment ago and nobody came that way."

Even as she spoke she saw on the worn rug on the floor between her and the police officer that there was a spot of blood. She saw it without really looking down at it, without taking her eyes from the officer's face, but she knew without being told that it was incriminating evidence unless she could hide it.

She stepped forward, covered it with her foot and pointed, as she did so, to the money on the bed.

"If any criminal had come in here," she said, "do you imagine he would have left that behind?"

The three men looked at the money and then back at Melina.

"He is not a thief," the police officer said briefly. "I have my orders. This room must be searched."

He snapped his fingers and the two Moroccans moved forward to open the wardrobe where Melina's few dresses were hung and the cupboard which held nothing except her two small suitcases.

It was then that the police officer walked towards the bathroom door. He turned the handle. The door was locked.

"Who is in there?"

His voice was almost drowned by the sudden rush of water. Someone had turned on both the bath taps full

15

blast. The police officer knocked on the door. There was no answer. It was doubtful if the occupant inside could hear him above the noise of rushing water.

He knocked again, this time more thunderously, and now the taps were turned off and a voice asked:

"What do you want, darling?"

The police officer turned towards Melina.

"Who is in there?" he inquired again.

"My . . . my husband."

Melina told the lie and felt the blood rush accusingly to her cheeks. The police officer looked at her for a moment and she felt that he did not believe her.

"Your husband!"

He looked round the tidy bedroom. It did not look like a room that was being shared. There were no clothes belonging to a man either in the wardrobe or on the chair.

"Your husband!" he repeated reflectively. "He is staying here with you?"

"As a matter of fact," Melina answered, "he has only just arrived. I was not expecting him, but he turned up. He . . . he came by plane."

Again she could see that the police officer was not inclined to believe her.

"I should like to speak to your . . . husband," he said grimly.

He hammered on the bathroom door.

"Come out, if you please."

"Who's there?" came the question.

"The police. Kindly open the door. We wish to question you."

"Question me? Good Lord, darling! What have you been up to?"

The voice was the gay, unconcerned voice of an Englishman who has nothing to fear and believes that the police are only concerned with the parking of a car or the fact that one has left it without the lights on.

"They . . . they are looking for a man," Melina said.

She somehow felt that she had to take part in this strange drama. At the same time, she knew that her

16

hands were trembling a little. The man, as she had first seen him, had looked so villainous with the blood on his face and on the knife he held in his hand. What had he done? Whom was she helping to evade justice?

It flashed through her mind that now she was hopelessly involved. There would be a case and she would have to give evidence. She would have to explain to a jury in a crowded court why she had championed a man who had dropped on to her balcony, obviously fleeing from justice, obviously an assailant of some sort.

Why couldn't she have had the sense to tell him to run to somewhere else in the hotel and then directed the other men after him? But she told herself he was English! She would expect to be helped if she appealed to one of her fellow-countrymen abroad, and she must do the same.

"Well, give me a moment," she heard the voice say from behind the bathroom door. "Tell whoever is there that I'm having a bath. Offer them a drink or something."

"I'm afraid I haven't got any drink up here," Melina answered resisting an absurd desire to giggle hysterically.

It was all so ridiculous, she thought; just like a rather bad film. And yet the knives in the hands of the two Moroccans were real enough and so was the pistol in the belt of the police officer.

"I do not suppose my husband will be long," she said with an effort at unconcern and walking to the bed picked up the money that was lying on it.

To do so she had to pass very near the two Moroccans. They smelt of sweat and excitement and—something else. Something which made her remember the words of an old nanny she had had once.

"There's many kinds of smells," she had said, "and evil's the worst of them."

Yes, they were evil. Melina was sure of it. She gathered up her money, feeling, though she did not look at them, the eyes of the men were glinting enviously as she put it away in her handbag.

17

Then deliberately she forced herself to move to the looking-glass. She tidied her hair, patting it neatly over each ear.

"It's a nice day for my husband to arrive in Tangier," she said conversationaly to the police officer. "He has never been here before and I did so want him to see it at its best."

The men were looking at her uncertainly. She knew that her unconcern was making them uneasy and doubtful if they could really trust what they had seen with their own eyes.

As if agitated by his own thoughts, the police officer hammered again on the bathroom door.

"Open the door, please, sir. We cannot waste time waiting for you."

Melina noted the word "sir", and felt a sudden rise of hope in her heart. If only when they saw him they would not recognise him. If only somehow he had got rid of those bloodstained garments.

"I can't think what all the fuss is about," a lazy voice said and then the door was opened and he was standing there.

He was wearing the white towelling *peignoir* which the hotel provided not only for those who wanted to have a bath but for those who wished to go down and swim on the beach. Above it his face was very sunburnt, but his hair was fair and one side of his face had been newly shaved while the other was lathered with soap and in his hand he held the razor which Melina used to keep her legs smooth before she went swimming.

"Now, what's all this about?" he asked, looking with what Melina thought was quite unexaggerated surprise at the three men standing in the bedroom.

"My men saw a criminal we were chasing drop down on to this balcony," the police officer said, but now his voice was less aggressive and there was something not quite positive in his tone.

"Well, your men must have been mistaken, mustn't they?" the Englishman replied. "And what am I sup-

18

posed to do about it? He's not here in the bathroom with me, as you can see for yourself. Have you looked under the bed? My wife will tell you he certainly wasn't in the room when I went to my bath and she has been here ever since."

"There—must have been a mistake," the police officer mumbled.

"There must, indeed," the Englishman answered. "And hadn't you better be running about looking for him instead of standing here asking me a lot of questions I can't answer? If you will excuse me I will go back to my shaving."

He turned as he spoke towards the glass over the basin in the bathroom and started to move the razor with precision down his lathered cheek.

The police officer looked at his assistants. Melina did not understand what he said but the gist of his words was quite obvious. Fools and imbeciles that they were, they had let the man they were seeking slip through their fingers.

The police officer bowed to Melina.

"Your pardon, *Madame*. Good afternoon, *M'sieur*!"

Knowing that the other two men were watching her and that there was still a look of suspicion in their eyes, she turned unconcernedly back to the dressing-table and picking up a lipstick began to outline her lips.

She heard the door shut behind them and then she turned, only to see the Englishman at the open door of the bathroom with his finger to his lips. Then for a moment he disappeared and she heard the taps running again—a barrier of sound to prevent eavesdropping, she thought, before he walked back to her holding the white *peignoir* around him.

And now she saw that the lather had gone from the unshaven side of his face and there was a long scratch that was still bleeding slightly.

"Oh, your face!" she exclaimed involuntarily.

He smiled.

"My face doesn't matter," he said quietly. "I've got you to thank for saving my life!"

19

2

"I . . . don't understand what this is all about," Melina faltered.

The stranger smiled and she saw that now the blood was beginning to trickle down his cheek from which he had removed the lather.

"You're bleeding!"

"It's only a scratch," he replied.

"Is that what you call it?" she asked a little dryly, as she turned towards her dressing-table and taking some cleansing tissues from their box held them out to him.

Crossing to the mirror he began to wipe away the blood. It was undoubtedly a deep scratch, and without saying anything Melina handed him a small bottle of antiseptic which she always carried with her.

"I can see you are a very practical girl," he remarked as he took it from her.

"I am wondering if you ought to have a stitch or two in it," she said.

He shook his head.

"No doctors, I'm allergic to them!"

She watched him clean the wound; then he looked at her with a twinkle in his eyes and a raised eyebrow.

"No plaster?" he said. "Don't say you're going to fail me now."

She opened a drawer and found what he wanted and he covered the cut on his cheek and threw the blood-stained tissues into the wastepaper basket. Then, having done so, he bent down and took them out again.

"Never leave traces of the crime," he said lightly. "That's the first rule for all good criminals."

He went into the bathroom and she heard him flushing the stained tissues down the lavatory. She waited until he came back again into the room before she spoke.

"I don't understand," she said, repeating herself. "When you dropped down on to the balcony I was quite sure you were an Arab. Now please tell me what all this is about."

She knew as she spoke that her question embarrassed him. He looked away from her, walked a few steps towards the open window and then, with his back to her, said:

"I wish I could explain it all to you. As it is, I must simply ask you to take me on trust, a fellow-countryman in trouble—and you have helped me more than I can possibly begin to explain."

"Would they really have killed you?" Melina asked in a low voice.

"Perhaps they would only have locked me up," he replied, his voice deliberately careless, and she knew he was evading the question.

"But what have you done?"

He turned round laughingly.

"Isn't that like a woman?" he said. "You are already convinced it is my fault. What do you think I have done? Pinched some money out of the till or been bolder still and robbed a bank?"

"You wouldn't have had to be dressed as an Arab to do either of those things," Melina answered.

"You're being too curious," he said. "Quite frankly the main problem at the moment is how I am to get away from here."

"You mean without any clothes?" Melina said. "What about your Arab disguise?"

"It's rather wet at the moment," he replied almost apologetically. "I hid it in the cistern of the lavatory."

Melina laughed—she couldn't help it.

"It's all like a television serial," she said. "Quite frankly, if I hadn't taken such a dislike to those two men with the police officer I wouldn't believe a word of it. You're quite sure we haven't got a candid camera hidden somewhere in the walls?"

21

He looked at her reflectively for a moment and then he said:

"Walk out to the balcony. Stand looking at the view as if you are admiring it and then, as you turn to come back, glance up at the roof. Tell me if you can see anything."

Melina obeyed him without argument. She walked on to the balcony, stood for a moment staring at the blue sea, the sunshine on the white roofs and an aeroplane winging its way in from Gibraltar. Then, a little self-consciously because she knew he was watching her, she turned back towards the bedroom. She glanced up. A head ducked behind the parapet but not before she had seen and noted the headdress.

"There is an Arab on the roof to the left," she said. "He ducked down when he saw me."

"That is what I was expecting," the stranger said. "And now will you open your bedroom door. Look down the corridor and tell me if there is anyone about."

Feeling as if she was acting in some strange and rather frightening charade, Melina did as she was asked. At the far end of the long, narrow corridor an Arab was sitting cross-legged on the floor, presumably asleep. She re-entered the room and closed the door behind her.

"There is someone else there," she said. "And I don't think it's one of the hotel servants."

"Charming, isn't it?" he said. "A prisoner in a white bathrobe. Now let me think what we do about this."

"Surely you can tell me what all this is about?" Melina said. "I don't think it's fair to come in here and frighten me without letting me understand. . ."

She stopped suddenly. There was a knock on the door. She saw the expression on the stranger's face and knew what he expected.

"Go into the bathroom," she whispered.

She heard him turn the key in the lock. She waited for a moment, trying to control her breathing which

22

was coming quickly from between her lips. Then the knock came again.

"Who . . . who is it?" she asked and knew that her voice quavered.

"It's I, Ambrose!" was the answer, and in the relief of its being someone she knew Melina ran the few steps to the door and flung it wide.

"Mr. Wheatley!" she said. "I wasn't expecting you."

She had never smiled at him in such a charming manner before, but the relief that he was not a bloodthirsty Arab made her forget her caution where Mrs. Schuster's young friend was concerned.

Ambrose came into the room and shut the bedroom door behind him.

"I say, Melina," he said. "I've just heard that you've got the sack. It's a damned shame if you ask me."

"It doesn't matter," Melina said, feeling suddenly that it was a very long time ago since she had got the sack and that at the moment Mrs. Schuster seemed far less real to her than the man in the bathroom and the danger that surrounded him.

Ambrose Wheatley could help, she thought.

"I have never heard such a thing as to turn you off just like that," Ambrose Wheatley was saying. "But then my cousin was always a hard woman, we know that. She's too attractive, has got too much money and, most important, she's an American. They always think in that country that God made the world for American women to use as a footstool, and your late employer for one cannot bear to think she can't get her own way in everything."

"I think she usually does, doesn't she?" Melina said vaguely, not really interested for the moment in Mrs. Schuster.

"Now look here," Ambrose Wheatley said, coming closer to her and putting his hand on her shoulder. "I feel this is partly my fault. I'm afraid I showed rather too obviously how jolly pretty I think you are—in fact you're far too attractive for any normal man's peace of mind. So, I've got an idea. Will you listen to it?"

23

"Yes . . . yes, I suppose so," Melina said.

When he had first appeared, she had been about to blurt the predicament of the Englishman who was hiding in her bathroom. Now, as she had been unable to get a word in because Ambrose Wheatley had so much to say, she was beginning to have second thoughts.

She had thought it would be easy to enlist his help, but now she was beginning to see not only that the story sounded a very fishy one, but how was she to explain the presence of a strange man whose name she did not even know, dressed in her white *peignoir* and hiding behind the locked door of the bathroom?

"What I am going to suggest," Ambrose Wheatley went on, "may sound a little peculiar to you to start with. But if you agree I am quite sure we will find it will be the hell of a lot of fun together."

"What is it?" Melina asked, her mind almost fully occupied with the question of whether she should tell him or whether she shouldn't.

"Well, the truth is," Ambrose Wheatley said, "I can't afford to quarrel with my cousin because she's promised to finance a little invention of mine: at the same time, I don't want to see you carted on my account. So I thought that, if you'd agree, you could stay on in Morocco—I'll find the money for that somehow—and we could meet whenever I was off duty so to speak."

He coughed as if embarrassed by what he was saying.

"We've booked at all the best hotels," he went on, "as you well know, but there are other ones—quiet little affairs round the corner where you would be quite comfortable—and when she lies down in the afternoons or when she's gone to bed, I'll pop out and we'll enjoy ourselves. What do you say to that?"

Melina stared at him in astonishment. She had always thought he was conceited and somewhat of a cad but she had never believed that he would suggest anything quite so outrageous or so humiliating.

She shook herself free of the hand on her shoulder and said icily:

24

"I am afraid, Mr. Wheatley, I am not very good at backstairs intrigues."

"Now, Melina, don't take it like that," he pleaded. "You know as well as I do that I can't say, 'Keep this girl as your secretary. I've got a liking for her and I want to see her around.' Besides, I personally have got too much at stake at the moment."

"And so have I," Melina said. "I've got my reputation and my self-respect. I think you flatter yourself, Mr. Wheatley. I'm not the least bit interested in you as a man and I never have been."

He blinked his eyes and she felt he couldn't have been more astonished if she had slapped him in the face. He was good looking in a rather theatrical manner and there were no doubt dozens of women who would find him irresistible. He was, in fact, with his good manners and sophisticated conversation the typical Mayfair young man who took up jobs such as decorating, trying to patent some inventions or pioneering exhibitions of unknown French artists, and used his social connections to finance them himself.

He had been to a good public school, belonged to several of the best clubs, could dance well and was used to any advances he made to the opposite sex being received with enthusiasm.

"I say, do you really mean that?" Ambrose Wheatley expostulated now in almost shocked surprise.

The penny had really dropped in his brain that Melina disliked him and yet he could hardly believe his senses.

"Yes, I do," she said.

"Very well, then," he replied huffily. "If you don't want my help, I only hope you'll find it easy to get back home. My cousin told me you had nothing but a week's wages between you and starvation—but perhaps she had forgotten there are other ways of earning one's living."

The implication in his sneering voice was quite plain and Melina resisted the impulse to throw something at

25

him. He walked out of the room and slammed the door behind him.

Yet as soon as he had gone she wanted to call him back. It was all very well to be proud, but she might at least have borrowed something from him for her fare to England. She had really forgotten until this moment her plan to go humbly to the British Consulate and ask their help.

The door of the bathroom opened.

"You were magnificent," a quiet voice said. "It was very difficult for me not to come out and kick him. I would have done just that if I had had any shoes on."

Melina laughed. The thought of Ambrose Wheatley being kicked hard by this strong, wiry man was a pleasant one.

"Is it true?" the stranger asked.

"Is what true?" Melina inquired.

"What he said about you being sacked and left here without any money?"

"Unfortunately it is," Melina said lightly. "But I am going to the British Consulate. I believe they help stranded women under these circumstances."

The stranger sat down on one of the beds.

"I've got a better idea," he said.

"What is it?" Melina asked.

"That you should work for me," he said. "I'm very much in need of you at the moment."

"I'm afraid I shan't be able to offer you a very good reference," Melina said with a smile. "Mrs. Schuster, my late employer, said I was both incompetent and impertinent."

"What was the real trouble?" he inquired. "Not our friend Mr. Wheatley?"

Melina nodded, amused by his perception.

"I'm afraid so," she said. "Mrs. Schuster took a liking to him."

"And he took a liking to you," the stranger added. "Oh, well, it's a story that I seem to have heard before somewhere."

"Everything seems like a fairy tale at the moment,"

Melina said. "Mrs. Schuster, Ambrose Wheatley and you! You are none of you real characters. Either you are all mad and I am sane or I am raving and should be locked up—I really don't know which!"

"Does it matter?" the man on the bed asked. "You're in the middle of an adventure, that's all. Isn't it rather better than hammering a typewriter in Whitehall, or wherever you did it before?"

"Hampstead," Melina said automatically; then glancing towards the sunshine outside the window, she went on: "Yes, much better. I have wanted to come here all my life and now I can hardly believe it's true that I've seen it."

"And where were you going with Mrs. Schuster? Marrakesh?" the stranger inquired.

"That's right. I have dreamed about that too! I've seen Winston Churchill's paintings and I've collected photographs of it ever since I was a child. And now I suppose through my own stupidity I shall miss it."

"Your own stupidity?"

"What else can I blame?" Melina said. "I ought to have dragged my hair back into a bun and worn dark glasses over my eyes the very first moment Ambrose Wheatley appeared. It isn't that he's really interested in me; he'll never be interested in anyone but himself. But he's just so conceited that he thinks every woman is fair game."

"You're making me regret those shoes," the stranger said. "Now, if only I'd had my army boots with me what a difference that would have made."

Melina laughed again. It was so ridiculous somehow. Here was this man she had never seen before seated comfortably on her bed and talking nonsense, while outside there were sinister Arabs waiting, apparently, to kill or imprison him.

With an effort she tried to be sensible.

"Listen," she said. "We cannot go on gossiping here. If you're in real danger, the first thing you've got to have is clothes, that's obvious. How can we get them for you?"

27

"The first thing," the stranger replied, "is for you to accept my offer of employment. Whatever that woman Mrs. Schuster was giving you I'm quite sure it wasn't enough and I can make it more. Secondly, she wanted to get rid of you and I need you desperately. I somehow think that might count."

He was almost too clever, Melina thought. He could see—or was she imagining it?—something of the loneliness which had been hers ever since her father died; her longing to be wanted; her dreams in which she did something worthwhile for somebody who really mattered. And yet because she was a little frightened of him she played for time.

"I suppose you realise that I don't even know your name?" she said.

"I know yours," he replied. "It's Melina—and a very pretty name too. Have you got another one?"

"Most people have two," she answered. "It's Lindsay, if you want to know."

"Melina Lindsay! Charming!"

"And yours?"

She thought he hesitated a moment as if he was going to lie and then he told her the truth.

"My name is Ward," he said. "Not a very exciting name, but my parents—in a misguided attempt, I think, to make it sound interesting—christened me Benjamin. It is not a name I ever allow anyone to use, so my friends, and most of my enemies, too, call me Bing. Now we're introduced."

"How do you do?" Melina said. "And thank you for your offer of a job. I'm very pleased to accept—so long as you can assure me that I shan't find a knife between my shoulders one dark night."

"I can't promise you anything of the sort," Bing answered, and to her surprise his voice was serious.

He rose to his feet, walked to the window and then back again across the room.

"I ought not to ask this of you," he said. "It's wrong and it's definitely against my principles and you may easily, as you put it, end up with a knife between your

28

shoulders. And yet it seems as if it was providence finding you. Out of all the balconies of the hotel that I might have dropped on to I had to choose yours."

"If you are trying to frighten me I don't think I am easily frightened," Melina said. "If taking employment with you means that I can stay in Morocco, then I am prepared to risk almost anything to do that."

"You'll stay in Morocco," he answered. "The difficulty will be to get out of the country."

He turned to face her and she thought that where before his eyes had seemed blue, now they were grey and steel-like.

"It wouldn't be right for me to let you work for me unless you knew what you were facing," he said. "I am a wanted man. I'm in the devil of a hole at the moment, as you can see for yourself. Somehow I shall get out of it because up till now my luck has always held. That is why I feel you are lucky for me. It wouldn't have happened this way if it hadn't been meant."

The sternness of his face relaxed and he smiled.

"It may seem nonsense to you," he said, "but I have lived too long in the East not to believe in fate, Karma, anything you like to call it; or as the Arabs say—'What will be, will be'. You happened along and from an entirely selfish point of view I cannot afford to let you go."

Melina stared at him. He was not as young as she had thought at first. There were deep lines in his face, lines perhaps of tiredness, or exertion, but also lines of experience. There was something about him which made her want to trust him.

He was not exactly handsome; in fact she thought to herself suddenly he had a hard, almost cruel face except when he was smiling. And yet unlike Ambrose Wheatley, she could not imagine him doing a mean or underhand thing. He might be hard, ruthless, at the same time he would be straight.

"It is crazy," she thought to herself. "Crazy to feel one can trust a stranger, a man about whom one knows nothing." And yet aloud she said:

29

"Thank you for telling me what you have, but I should like to work for you."

"Very well," he answered. "And thank you. I can only hope that things won't be as bad as they might be."

He looked down at her and she dropped her eyes before his. There was something about his very seriousness which was vaguely embarrassing because she did not understand it. With an effort she forced herself to say lightly:

"Well, now I'm engaged what are your orders, sir?"

She saw him pucker his brow a little and square his jaw and guessed it was something he always did when he was concentrating, and then he said:

"I want you to go down to the reception desk and tell them that your husband has arrived unexpectedly."

Melina looked frightened.

"My . . . husband?" she faltered.

"Of course," he answered. "Didn't you realise you're engaged as my wife? We've already established that with the police officer. His report will by now have gone to headquarters."

"Your wife!" Melina said again. "I . . . I hadn't understood that."

Bing made a gesture of impatience.

"What does it matter," he said, "what you call yourself? My wife, my secretary, my driver! We have got to be together. The men who came here believe that we are married. It is going to be rather difficult to present them with a different story."

"Yes, yes, of course," Melina agreed.

"Very well, then," Bing went on in a matter-of-fact voice which somehow seemed to make it sound better. "Tell the reception desk that your husband has arrived unexpectedly and that you will be checking out this afternoon. What about your bill?"

"Mrs. Schuster is paying that at the end of the week," she said.

"That's all right then. If they charge extra for my having used the bath she can pay for it," Bing smiled.

"After you've spoken to the reception desk I want you to go into the telephone booth in the hall, be quite certain the door is shut and then ring up this number I will give you."

He looked round the room for a piece of paper and a pencil. There was a Biro lying on the dressing-table and taking a tissue from the box where Melina kept them he wrote a number on it.

"A man will answer," he said. "Just say 'I'm speaking from the Excelsior Hotel; the Sahib has need of you'."

"The Sahib has need of you," Melina repeated. "Will he understand?"

"He will understand," Bing said. "Be careful to speak straight into the mouthpiece so that nobody watching can read your lips."

"Who is likely to be able to lip-read here?" Melina asked in astonishment.

"Some of the men waiting in the hall are very good at it," Bing answered. "When you have finished go back to the reception desk and say your husband's luggage will be arriving during the afternoon."

Melina drew a deep breath.

"Anything else?" she inquired.

"Well, now I think of it," Bing answered, "I could do with something to eat. I haven't had anything since last night."

"Good Heavens!" Melina exclaimed. "You must be starved. What would you like?"

"I don't want the waiter to come in here while you're away," he said reflectively, "or, for that matter, even when you're here."

"Shall I slip outside and buy something?" Melina suggested. "There's a shop opposite—a store that sells all sorts of food."

"Get me anything," he said, "but have it packed so that no one can recognise what it is."

"Leave that to me," Melina said.

She picked up her bag.

"I'm afraid you will have to finance me," Bing said,

"until my servant arrives. Oh, and by the way, I forgot to say one thing. When you say, 'the Sahib has need of you', add the number of your room."

"They may ask your name at the desk," Melina said. "What shall I say?"

"May I borrow your name for the moment?" Bing asked with a smile. "I rather fancy Lindsay!"

"I think it will save complications," Melina said. She wandered to the door and then turned and looked back.

"Are you sure you will be here when I return?" she asked. "I have a feeling that I am dreaming all this and when I wake up there will be nothing for me to do but go tamely and call on the British Consul."

"I cannot promise you anything but that what lies ahead is certainly not going to be tame," Bing answered.

"Now you are employing me," Melina said, "won't you tell me what it's all about?"

"Honestly, I think it's better for you to know nothing," he replied. "Besides, it's not my secret."

"In other words the answer is no," Melina said.

"It would sound rather rude if I put it so abruptly," he said with a smile.

She turned away disappointed. As she reached the passage, she heard the key turn in the lock of the door behind her and then she walked quickly down the corridor. She passed the Arab at the end of it. He was pretending to be asleep, but she was quite sure he was watching her beneath his eyelids. She had a sudden glimpse of a knife tucked into his waist.

"What have I let myself in for?" she asked herself as she waited for the lift. "I should have done the sensible thing and gone home." And yet she knew she was only giving her conscience lip-service. She had no intention of going home. It was far too exciting even though she could not help a sudden pricking at the base of her skull, a sudden flutter within her breast.

What was this man up to? And why were they after him? She knew that she could never rest until she

32

learned the answer to the problem. At the same time she was sure that it would be no use trying to coax him into telling her. He was not that type of man. If he wanted to keep a secret, he would keep it and nothing she could say or do would alter his decision.

She told the man at the desk that her husband had arrived unexpectedly. He was extremely disinterested, knowing her only to be the servant of Mrs. Schuster and therefore not in any way a valuable client of the hotel.

She wondered why Bing had wanted her to make this explanation. And then she had the quick impression that someone at the back of her, someone amongst the number of people standing about in the foyer or sitting waiting on the benches provided for the page boys and guides, was listening to what was being said. That was why he wanted her to say it, she thought.

She moved from the reception desk to the telephone box. She went in, reached for the receiver and then realised that, while she was quite certain she had closed the door as she entered, it was already ajar. There was an Arab with his back to her standing outside. She could see his robes. She pulled the door closed again and fastened it firmly. Now the kiosk was hot and airless, but it was sound-proof.

She lifted the receiver, dialled the number Bing had given her and heard it ringing; then someone lifted the receiver at the other end. Whoever it was did not speak, but she could hear him breathing.

"I am speaking from the Excelsior Hotel; the Sahib has need of you. Room three hundred and nine."

There was no answer, only the sound of the telephone receiver being replaced.

Melina came out of the box, the Arab who stood outside had disappeared. She went out of the hotel and crossed the road to the delicatessen shop. She had a feeling she was being followed, but it might have been entirely her imagination.

The shop was full of women making purchases. Most of them were tourists—English, Italian or Ger-

33

man—and Melina had the feeling that there was nothing sinister about any of them. But they sampled goods, changed their minds and asked for fruit and vegetables which required weighing, so it was a long time before she could get anyone to serve her.

When at last she was asked what she required, she bought a loaf of crisp, French bread, some butter, ham, sausage and cheese, and half a dozen tangerines with the leaves still attached to them. She persuaded the shopkeeper to put them all in a large, brown-paper bag and slung it over her arm, hoping that it would look like some casual purchases of no special importance.

Then striving to appear in no particular hurry, stopping to glance in two or three shop windows on the way, she walked back to the hotel. She felt as if eyes were boring into her back as she walked across the foyer and was taken up in the lift.

The Arab was still dozing in the corner of the corridor and she noted that he was out of sight of the lift and that, as usual, there were no servants about to serve these unimportant rooms on the top floor of the hotel.

She paused for a moment outside her own door, wondering if what she had half anticipated would happen had done so and Bing had already gone. Perhaps she had dreamt him and the whole incredible episode. Then she knocked and heard his voice say:

"Who's there?"

"It's me, Melina," she replied ungrammatically.

She heard the key turn. She opened the door and saw to her surprise that he was dressed. He was wearing an old grey flannel suit, a clean white shirt with a dark blue tie and had a pair of comfortable leather slippers on his feet. She looked round for a suitcase and saw none.

"Your servant was very quick," she exclaimed.

"Very," he agreed.

"Your clothes must have been quite near here."

"Now you're being curious," he said, "and I'm dying of hunger."

34

"I'm sorry," she replied. "I only hope I've brought you something you will like."

She took out the contents of her bag and put them on the small table.

"A feast for the gods!" he exclaimed.

"I didn't know whether to bring you anything to drink," she answered.

"The tangerines will be quite enough," he said. "And now will you forgive me if I stop talking and stuff myself? I really am hungry."

She felt almost maternal as she watched him buttering the bread and stuffing it into his mouth, eating the ham with his fingers and following it with cheese which he sandwiched between two pieces of buttered crust.

Finally he gave a little sign as if in repletion.

"I wouldn't have exchanged that meal for all the caviar in Russia," he said.

"What do we do now?" Melina asked.

"Wait for a little longer," he answered. "I'm expecting a visitor."

"A visitor?"

"Yes," he answered. "But don't be nervous. It's no one of any importance—merely someone who is bringing us a car."

"Then we really are leaving today?" Melina said. "I had better start packing."

"I can give you about half an hour," he said. "In the meantime, will you object if I take a short sleep on your bed?"

"No, of course not," Melina said.

"Like my meals, my sleeping hours have been slightly erratic these last few days.

He lay down as he spoke, pulling the pillow behind his head, and then almost as if he switched out a light he was asleep. Melina stared at him in amazement. She had never imagined that anyone could drop off so quickly and yet she had the feeling that should it be required of him he could as quickly awake and be instantly alert.

She took her suitcases from the cupboard and filled

35

them quickly. She had not many clothes with her, she had not been able to afford them, but what she had had been chosen with care.

Her clothes, she had thought, would be worthy of the land she longed to visit. Crisp, fresh, cotton dresses; two pretty, uncrushable evening dresses; a white coat to wear over them; shoes which she was wise enough to buy because they were comfortable rather than because they looked fashionable.

She was ready and everything was in her suitcase and still Bing slept on. There was a knock at the door and exactly as she had known would happen he was wide awake and sitting up almost before whoever had knocked could have taken their hand away.

"Ask who it is," he said almost under his breath.

"Who's there?" Melina inquired.

"A message for Mr. Lindsay!" a boy's voice replied.

Bing gave Melina a little imperceptive signal with his head to open the door. She saw him move back further into the room and his hand go to the pocket of his coat. She opened the door a little. Only a page-boy stood there.

"The car is waiting below, *Madame*," the boy said. "And here is a note for Mr. Lindsay."

She took it from him, found a small coin in her bag and gave it to him. He thanked her politely and walked away down the corridor. Before she could even shut the door Bing had taken the envelope from her and torn it open.

Without really realising she did so she looked over his shoulder. Only two words were written on the piece of paper that he opened: *"Villa Harris"*.

The words seemed somehow to please him. He thrust the paper and the envelope into his pocket and picked up her suitcases.

"Come along," he said.

"But your luggage!" she cried.

"I've got everything I want," he answered with a smile and she knew that somehow the information had merely been of interest to whoever was listening when

36

she told the man at the reception desk that her husband had arrived and that his luggage would be coming later.

Parked immediately outside the hotel was a small, grey Peugeot. Bing put Melina's luggage on the back seat and helped her in to the front. Then he got behind the wheel.

It seemed to Melina that no one even glanced at them as they drove off; and yet she felt from her own point of view that she was doing something so eccentric, so outrageous and extraordinary that everyone must stand and look.

Without saying good-bye, without even notifying the hotel that she was leaving, Melina Lindsay was driving away with a strange man she had never met until a few hours ago, a man of whom she knew nothing, a man who seemed to be taking part in an extremely dangerous and frightening mission also of which she knew nothing. A man, moreover, who had just engaged her to play the part of his wife!

They moved off into the busy traffic of the main street and then, as Bing put the grey car into top gear, he leaned back in his seat and turned to glance at her small, serious face.

"Enjoying yourself, Mrs. Ward?" he asked.

3

They left the crowded streets behind and started to climb a small hill behind the town on which Melina could see there was a white villa surrounded by a high wall.

Bing pointed to it with his finger.

"Villa Harris!" he said. "Built by an Englishman who was a correspondent of *The Times*. He is dead now and the Moroccans have made it one of the landmarks of the town and tourists are taken out to look at it—from the outside, of course."

"No one is allowed in?" Melina asked, disappointed.

Bing shook his head.

"You're lucky if you can get inside any of the buildings in Tangier once they are owned by the natives," he said. "They rather object to being stared at; and who doesn't?"

"I should like to go inside a real Moroccan house," Melina said.

Bing did not answer; he was intent on passing a number of small boys who were playing ball at the corner of the street in imminent danger of their lives.

"You must have been in a great many," Melina continued.

"What makes you think that?" Bing asked.

"When you are dressed as an Arab, surely you can go into Arab houses?" Melina ventured.

She knew she was being curious and was not unprepared for the little sidelong glance that Bing gave her and the twist of his lips as he said:

"*Les jeux sont faits, Madame.*"

It was the cry of the croupier at every casino when

38

no one may stake any more money because the ball is rolling in the roulette wheel.

Melina knew with a sense of exasperation that Bing had seen through her idea of making him talk and she sat back silent in the seat until Bing stopped the car below the Villa.

"We walk from here," he said. "It's too rough for my tyres."

She had a feeling, though she could not put it into words, that there were other reasons for his wishing to walk.

Obediently she climbed out into the hot sun, shaking the skirt of her cotton dress to prevent it from being creased and being glad, when she saw the rough stones and sand on what was little more than a cart-track, that she was wearing low-heeled sandals.

As they rounded the high white walls, the view over the sea was breathtaking. There were few people about, for it was the time of siesta and Melina knew that most of the Moslems would be asleep in their houses or drowsing over their wares in the market-place until the heat of the afternoon abated a little.

"Mad dogs and Englishmen . . ." she said aloud and Bing turned to smile at her.

"It isn't hot yet," he said. "Besides, I like the sun, don't you?"

"I can't really answer that question," Melina said. "I've never been in a hot country until now."

"Morocco is not really hot," Bing replied. "You should try India, the Persian Gulf or Aden in June. And even Algiers, next door, can be uncomfortably warm in the summer months."

He was talking casually enough, but Melina knew that his eyes were moving ahead of them, searching the stumpy trees and rocks and even a camping ground which was a little farther on, as if he was expecting to see something unusual.

The stony ground slipped beneath their feet and still they climbed. There were two children in charge of the three small, thin goats grazing a little above them.

39

Below them the ground fell away until they reached one point in the hillside where there was a sheer drop down hundreds of feet of rough, shaly cliff.

There were a few trees growing along the side and a broken down fence that had once prevented cars, and perhaps people, from running over the edge in the dark. The leaves of the trees were thick and dark in colour and silhouetted against the sky they made a picture which Melina somehow felt would be engraved on her mind.

Everywhere she looked she saw a lovelier scene than the last. It was hard to believe that only an hour or so earlier Bing had been pursued by men intent on violence or worse.

"You were expecting someone to meet you here?" Melina asked in a low voice.

"Perhaps," Bing said enigmatically.

"There doesn't seem anyone about," Melina said. "I can see some tents at the end of the camping ground. They look to me rather like those used by boy scouts."

Bing turned in the direction she pointed and with his back to the cliff searched with narrowed eyes the long, grassy incline where the boys were playing with the goats. There was a monument of some sort in the distance; a memorial perhaps; nothing more sinister.

"What do we do now?" Melina asked.

She turned her face up to his as she spoke and even as she did so she saw a slight movement in the tree behind him. If she had not been expecting trouble, and in consequence been tense and on edge, she would not have screamed so quickly. As it was her scream made Bing swing round just in time to catch the man who had sprung at his back. He was an Arab and he held a knife in his hand!

After the first scream had left her lips Melina felt paralysed and unable to move. She could only stand breathless and watch Bing struggling with the man who, although smaller in height, was fighting fanatically.

As he jumped, Bing had caught hold of the man's right wrist and though he kicked and clawed and strug-

40

gled he was unable to use the long, pointed knife which gleamed in the sunshine or strike as he had intended.

They struggled in silence, the only sound being the scuffle of their feet on the gravel. Then almost before Melina could realise what was happening Bing picked up the man bodily in both his arms. For a second he held him high above his head before he flung him over the battered fence and down the deep, stony ravine.

There was one cry, the sound of a thud and a shower of stones as the body fell over and over, bashing itself against the rocks as it fell—and then silence.

There was sweat on Bing's face as he turned towards Melina, but there was something else which made her take a step backwards from him, a new feeling she had never known before seeping through her as if she, herself, had received a knife in her heart.

His face was transformed. No longer was it the face of a quiet, pleasant Englishman, but the face, she told herself, of a devil. There was a glint in his eyes, a cruel twist to his mouth, the set of his jaw and, above all, an expression of satisfaction, of triumph.

It was then, instinctively, that she began to run— running away from him, her feet scurrying over the stony, sandy path as her terror urged her on until, passing the Villa Harris, she found herself back again at the car.

The run had exhausted her and without thinking coherently that it was Bing's car yet also Bing from whom she was escaping, she leant against it panting, holding on with her hands to one of the side mirrors although after being in the sun the chromium seemed to burn her as if it were on fire.

She heard him come up behind her and without looking up she managed to gasp:

"Let . . . me . . . go! I cannot . . . stay with . . . you. Let me . . . go!"

"Pull yourself together!"

He spoke sharply and opened the door of the car.

"Get in," he said.

41

"I can't. I'll . . . I'll . . . walk back," Melina managed to gasp.

"Get in!"

His voice was inexorable and she obeyed him simply because she no longer had breath with which to argue. She sank down in the seat and put her hands up to her eyes. She couldn't look at him; she couldn't bear to see that expression on his face.

Why had she been such a fool to come here with this man—this killer who enjoyed the killing? In a kind of agony she heard him open the door next to the driver's seat. Then, as she expected him to get into the car, she heard him pause.

There was a child's voice speaking to him in Arabic; begging, no doubt, for money in the traditional way or presenting a nosegay of wild flowers which he had picked on the hillside. Bing was feeling in his pocket and then, in an ordinary, conversational voice that any husband might have used to his wife he said:

"Have you got any small change?"

With trembling hands, fighting back the tears which were now pricking her eyes, Melina opened her bag. She pulled out her small purse and handed it to him and knew that he took a coin out of it and gave it to the boy before he got into the car and tossed a little nosegay of flowers on to her lap.

"Thank you," he said, giving the purse into her nervous hand.

With an effort she forced herself to put her purse away and then realised he had not started up the car but was just sitting in it. She turned her face away from him looking blindly out of the window beside her.

"Melina, look at me!"

"I don't . . . want to."

She knew it was the reply of a sulky child but somehow she felt peculiarly childlike at this moment.

"Melina, don't be silly. These things have to be done. You've got to understand. Besides, I owe you a debt of gratitude."

Still she did not answer and he went on:

"It was him or me! If you hadn't screamed that knife would have been buried in my back—and you would have had a lot of explaining to do as to why your 'husband' should have been killed by some religious fanatic beside the Villa Harris on a quiet afternoon when everything else seemed at peace."

"How ... could you ... do it?" Melina asked. "Wasn't there ... any other way?"

"Melina, look at me," he repeated, and when she did not obey him he put out his hand and taking her small chin in his fingers turned her face round to his.

For a moment she resisted him and then, compelled almost against her will, her eyes opened and looked up into his. Could any man look like that, she wondered involuntarily, and yet be a killer?

"It had to be done," he said quietly. "As I have told you, it was him or me. There was nothing else for it."

"But why did he want to ... kill you?" Melina asked.

She saw a sudden blankness come over his face and knew that he was going to refuse to answer the question.

"You've got to tell me!" she cried passionately. "Don't you understand? I can't go on? I can't stay with you unless you tell me the truth. I've got to know. You have said that I helped you, saved your life, if you like. Well, don't you owe me something? It's only frankness and honesty I'm asking for, nothing else. Just to know, just to understand what it is all about."

He took his hand away from her chin and turned to look out over the sunlit hillside. The boy who had brought the flowers was back again beside the goats. There was no one else in sight. It seemed utterly peaceful, quiet and serene.

"Tell me! Please tell me!" Melina begged.

"How can I be sure that I can trust you?" Bing answered. "It is not my secret. It would be so easy for you to walk out on me, as you were trying to do just now. There could be a word here or a word there and Heaven knows what would not be involved."

43

"You can trust me," Melina said briefly. "Perhaps I should have told you before. My father was Sir Frederick Lindsay!"

She saw Bing's eyes widen almost incredulously.

"Sir Frederick Lindsay! The man who did so much in Morocco! Good Lord! Why didn't you say so? I met him once, years ago, when I left school. But all he has done, his books, the stories about him, mean more to me than I can ever say."

"And yet he died penniless and without anybody apparently caring a damn one way or the other," Melina said bitterly. "He was very ill for the last three years of his life and none of the people who wrote such glowing obituaries ever bothered to ring up, or to write, or to come to see him. He would have appreciated it so much, but they just weren't interested when he was no longer of any importance."

"Your father will always be of importance," Bing said, "I can promise you that. His fight against the slave trade; his battle to prevent narcotics being brought into the country; the work he did to bring peace to Morocco. All this is something which those who write history will never forget, even if the Moroccans themselves may be somewhat grudging in their appreciation of his efforts."

"He didn't want to be thanked," Melina said quickly. "But I minded for him. He used to talk of Morocco as if it was his best beloved child. That is why I wanted to come here; that is why I wanted to see the country to which he had given his heart."

"You shall see it," Bing said. "But only if you've got some of his courage."

"Then tell me what I am fighting," Melina said.

Bing looked round over his shoulder as if he half expected there was someone crouching against the car listening to them.

"It's a long story," he said, "and I'm not going to bother you with the details, but your father fought all his life to improve conditions in Morocco and the new King has carried on the good work. He has closed

44

down innumerably many dens of vice; he has broken up secret societies; he has eliminated, in one way or another, a great number of perpetrators of evil—but not all of them."

Again Bing glanced over his shoulder.

"Naturally," he went on, "these people are not pleased at the new regime. They have been working against the King for a long time, and though they have not come into the open, those concerned with the government of the country know there is a vast underground movement ready at the first opportunity to sabotage and hinder every effort at improvement."

"You mean a revolution?" Melina asked.

"I don't think it will come to that," Bing answered, "for they are not strong enough, as yet, to show their hand. And if those who serve the King are really vigilant they never will."

"Go on," Melina prompted. "How are you concerned in this?"

"These people, who have no name, no badge and who work secretly, are all the more dangerous because no one knows where one may find them."

"The man who was in the tree—why should he want to kill you?"

"Who knows who gave him the order to strike at me? All I am certain of is that when his body is found nothing will be said. It will be taken away and buried, but little will be said about it except perhaps in the gossip markets and there will be nothing in the newspapers."

"It sounds frightening!" Melina murmured.

"It is frightening," Bing replied. "But I am not concerned with the revolutionaries—if one might call them that—as a whole; but only with one act of theirs."

"And what is that?" Melina asked.

Bing looked round. Everything was quiet and peaceful and there was only the sunlight outside.

"They have kidnapped a child," he said at length in a low voice.

"A child!" Melina exclaimed. "What child?"

45

"The child belonging to a friend of mine," Bing answered. "He was at Harrow with me and I came out here to stay with him. I have worked in these parts before in various capacities, but this time I came to Morocco for a holiday—a rest."

His lips twisted in a wry smile.

"I hadn't really started to relax!"

"Who is this man?" Melina asked.

"I am not going to tell you his name," Bing told her. "It is of no importance to you as things are and, quite frankly, I want you to know as little as possible—just in case anyone should interrogate you."

"You mean they might kidnap me?" Melina asked.

"Not if I'm about," Bing replied simply. "At the same time, I've got to protect you—even though you are your father's daughter."

He put his hand over hers for a moment as it lay on her lap and she heard the respect in his voice and felt warm that someone cared so much for her father and remembered him.

"This friend of mine," Bing went on, "has a position of importance in the Government. He was instrumental in having two men, steeped in wickedness and crime, brought before a Court of Justice and sentenced to death. They are to be executed in a week's time."

Melina turned wondering eyes toward Bing.

"And the child?" she asked.

"The child will die, too, unless he pardons them," Bing answered. "Or unless by some miracle I can find the child."

"But why you? Hasn't he told the police?" Melina asked, only to feel her voice die away between her lips, knowing without being told what the answer would be.

"You must see that it would be impossible to make such a situation public," Bing explained. "It might precipitate the very thing that we are trying to avoid— the strengthening of the forces against the King; a rallying cry for all those working underground to sabotage the Government."

"Oh, I see!" Melina murmured.

46

"What they hoped would happen of course," Bing continued, "was that the Minister in question would proclaim his loss in the newspapers and say he was being blackmailed to save the two men who really deserve to die."

"But it doesn't seem possible that such things can happen today," Melina cried.

"Things like this are happening all over the world," Bing answered. "Sometimes they are reported in the papers, sometimes not. The worst crimes are usually never heard of except by those people who make it their business to know about them. Already my friend has, I believe, embarrassed and disquieted the Opposition a little because he has said nothing and has gone about his business, although his heart is breaking, without revealing the tragedy which is hidden in his home."

"And the child! Supposing they kill it!" Melina said.

"They won't do that until the last moment," Bing replied confidently.

"Is it a boy or a girl?"

"A boy, of course," Bing replied. "Which naturally enhances the value of the hostage in Moslem eyes. A boy of six. All we know is that he is hidden somewhere in this vast country—and I have got one week in which to find him!"

"But ... but surely it's impossible?" Melina said. "What can you do, working alone?"

"I am not alone. There are loyal, decent people amongst the poor, amongst the beggars—and even the goatherds! But they are frightened. They can only work surreptitiously. They are afraid of their own shadows, suspicious of their relatives, in case they should be on the other side."

His eyes were on the small boys seated by the goats on the hillside.

"That boy who brought these flowers," Melina said looking down at them on her lap. "He told you something, didn't he?"

Bing nodded.

"He brought a message from his father who was too

47

afraid and too wise to come himself. He may have known about the man hidden in the tree or he may not. Anyway, two people knew I was coming here—the man who tried to kill me and the man who had a message for me. Do you understand now how complex the situation is?"

"And brother shall turn against brother," Melina quoted beneath her breath. "I have heard my father say that when he was describing a civil war in one country or another."

"It is very true of the East," Bing said, "where men are truly brothers and yet become bitter and more dangerous enemies because their affection has been so great."

There was silence and then he said:

"Why did you run away?"

She did not answer but he put his hands on hers again and said:

"Tell me, Melina. We must have the truth between us if nothing else."

"It was . . . your face," she said almost in a whisper as the horror of it returned to her. "You . . . killed a man and you looked . . . pleased—no, more than that . . . triumphant."

"I was," Bing said quietly. "I was glad there was one less of them, one less perhaps, of those swine who are torturing a child of six!"

"Torturing!"

Melina said the word sharply. It had an almost medieval sound in her ears.

"Yes, torturing," Bing said. "They have threatened to flog him every day that the reprieve is not announced."

"Oh, no!"

Melina's voice was broken.

"Now do you understand?" Bing asked. "Now are you prepared to work with me?"

"But, of course! I was anyway. You had engaged me. But now . . . Oh, don't let's waste time here. Let us go and do something."

48

"We are going to Fez," Bing said. "That was the message I received from the little goatherd. 'That which you seek travels to Fez'."

He turned the car and started down the hill. There were a thousand questions Melina wanted to ask him, but somehow she felt that she had delayed him long enough.

As soon as they were out on the open road she realised that the Peugeot might look small and insignificant but it was obviously fitted with a large and powerful engine. They sped along, passing cars that were much bigger than theirs was, and making short work of the long, twisting road which led into the centre of the country.

"Are we likely to be followed?" Melina asked once.

"Anything is likely," he answered. "Besides, my changed appearance in your bathroom has not fooled them as we hoped."

"Why didn't they kill you even though I was there?" Melina asked.

"God knows!" he answered. "It depends very much on who is on the chase. Some people are rather half-hearted about murder. They are never quite certain that their employers will stand by them when there's any trouble. And, remember, a dead Englishman in an hotel with a witness to see who has done it is a very different thing from a dead Englishman on the hillside, murdered by a man whose face you would not have seen and who, as far as you were concerned, would have disappeared into thin air."

"If only one knew what they were like. If only they wore a uniform," Melina said desperately.

"It is what I have often thought to myself," Bing replied. "But they really have nothing in common except a desire to create chaos in a country which is just finding peace."

"Does the King know about the child?" Melina asked.

"Of course," Bing replied. "But he, too, is powerless. As I have told you, to bring this thing into the open might precipitate the one thing we are trying to avoid— an open revolt."

"The police; the army! Aren't they loyal?"

"We hope so, but we don't know," Bing replied.

Melina was silent, remembering the policeman who had come into her bedroom. There had been something unpleasant about him, she thought. He did not exude evil as the other two men had done, but he was definitely not trustworthy. She began to see the enormity of the task Bing had undertaken.

"Who are these people who are helping you?" she asked.

He shrugged his shoulders.

"Again I do not know," he said. "The ayah of the child; the servants who guarded him, were, we think, loyal and utterly devastated when he was snatched away from his governess as he went down to the beach to bathe. The men picked him up in their arms and carried him to a car. The woman was left staring after the car, screaming for help, but by the time anyone paid any attention to her it was out of sight. The child had vanished."

"It's terrifying! Absolutely terrifying!" Melina cried.

"I suppose really I ought not to have embroiled you in all this," Bing said reflectively. "But somehow it seemed such a Heaven sent opportunity. Now that I realise that our little subterfuge was fruitless I ought to send you back."

"Even if you tried I won't go," Melina said.

"Are you sure about that?" he said. "You were running away from me just now."

"It was because you frightened me," Melina said. "But now I understand."

"And you are no longer frightened of me?" he asked.

She hesitated before she answered. She was frightened of him, she thought, if she were truthful. There was something about him, something strong and ruthless, which made her feel uneasy and, yes, a little afraid.

He did not press her for an answer and she was thankful not to have to lie.

They stopped for a drink and something to eat in a small village. Melina wondered, as they were served attentively by the owner of the restaurant, whether they just appeared to him to be ordinary travellers or whether he already had information about them.

Everything seemed completely and utterly normal and she began to think that perhaps all that had happened before was a bad dream or something that had come out of her own imagination and had not, in fact, occurred at all.

Bing paid the bill and then casually said in French:

"I suppose you haven't seen some friends of ours come through in the last day or so? There would have seen two or three of them with a small boy. They'd be travelling, I think, in a big touring car. I half expected to meet them here today."

The man hesitated for a moment but only as if he was thinking rather than for any ulterior motive.

"There was a small boy with some men here yesterday," he said. "They stopped for a meal at midday. The child asked for milk, but I had only goats' milk and he didn't like it."

"That may have been them," Bing said casually. "My wife and I got held up with car trouble. Oh, well, we shall meet them later on I expect."

"If it was the same party," the proprietor continued, "the chauffeur said he was going to Fez. He asked me how many kilometres it was."

"And how far is it?" Bing asked. "We hope to stay there tonight."

"Only about eighty kilometres," the man answered. "You will be there soon after dark."

"Thank you very much."

Bing put his hand under Melina's arm and led her towards the car.

"Don't look round," he said. "And don't say anything until we're out of earshot."

She could hardly hear his words and she knew his

51

cool deliberation in looking at the tyres and polishing the windscreen before they set off was all an act put on to impress the proprietor.

"Do you think he suspected us?" she asked as soon as they had driven away.

"He sounded natural enough," Bing answered.

"We're only a day behind them," Melina said.

"They may not stay there though," Bing replied. He glanced at his watch. "We are about ten minutes from the restaurant. Look back now and see if anyone is following us."

The road behind them was long and dusty. There was no one in sight.

"Are there other roads?" Melina asked.

"This is the only main route from Tangier to Fez," Bing said. "The side roads are in a bad state and in many places are only negotiable by horses."

"That was why you were sure they had come this way?" Melina suggested.

"They would have wanted to get the child out of Tangier quickly," Bing said. "I thought that was what had happened, but I had to make sure."

"And you nearly got yourself killed in the process," Melina said, thinking of his sudden jump on to the balcony and the urgency of his whispered voice when he had asked her to save him.

"And now? What happens now?" she went on.

He did not answer.

"Fez is the largest native town in the whole of North Africa," Bing said. "But I have an idea where they will take him and we can only hope my idea is right."

His voice was slow and deliberate and without emotion. Melina looked at him quickly and said:

"What you are planning is dangerous, isn't it?"

"Everything is dangerous," Bing answered. "But they are risks that have got to be taken."

He gave a quick sigh and added:

"I ought never to have brought you, I see that now."

"I'm glad you did," Melina replied. "Very glad. I

want to help you save that child and somehow I'm not so afraid as I thought I should be."

He turned and gave her a fleeting smile.

"Your father's daughter!" he said. "Good girl!"

She felt a glow at his words and she was suddenly surprisingly happy.

"Thank you," she said in a grateful voice. Then impulsively she put out her hand and laid it on his arm. "I am so very glad I met you," she said, and meant it.

4

It was almost dark as they neared Fez. Just before they reached the town Bing turned the car into a side road and stopped.

"What are you going to do?" Melina asked curiously.

"First I am going to change the number plates of the car," he answered.

He stopped under an ancient tree standing by itself on the flat land. He opened the back of the car and she saw her two suitcases and nothing else. He put them down on the ground, touched some secret spring and a false back to the boot swung open and she saw inside there were a number of things, including another suitcase.

"You are full of surprises," she said a little wryly.

For the moment she had the idea that he was just a charlatan, a wandering conjuror who was ready to bemuse gullible people like herself with a lot of magic and prepared surprises. Then she remembered with a little shiver the man he had flung over the cliff and his face when he had turned from doing it. This was serious. There was no pretence about this.

Bing drew out a couple of number plates and with an expert hand detached those that were already on the car and replaced them with the others. Melina stood watching him.

"What is going to be our story now?" she inquired.

"I have a feeling that we may be a step ahead of our enemies," he replied. "They may not have caught up with the idea that we have come to Fez. I may be wrong, but something in my bones tells me that the man in the tree was there by chance. He was not expecting us but was only posted as a kind of sentry."

He stood by to admire his handiwork.

"The Opposition do that sort of thing," he went on. "Half the slumberers at the street corners or the beggars hanging round the fountains are there for a purpose, although one has no idea what it is until something happens."

"In which case," Melina said slowly, "they—whoever they may be—do not know we have come to Fez."

"That is something we have to take a chance on," Bing answered.

He pulled an old and battered suitcase out of the secret partition in the boot. It was covered with labels of a dozen different countries. He opened it and taking off his coat, shirt and tie, put on an American shirt worn outside his trousers, with an open neck and short sleeves. It was screamingly vulgar, with bright coloured flowers on a yellow ground.

He next produced a white cap of the type which Middle-West Americans usually affect while they are in Europe, and put a pair of dark glasses on his nose. He looked so completely American—and a rather inferior brand at that—that Melina stood laughing at him.

"I only hope your accent matches the get-up," she said.

"It will," he answered a little grimly.

"And me? What about me!" she asked.

"No disguise for you," he said, firmly shutting up his suitcase. "You're my English wife. Don't forget there may have been people who have seen you in Tangier. By the way, does anybody over here know that you are Sir Frederick Lindsay's daughter?"

"I told Mrs. Schuster when she engaged me," Melina said. "But she had never heard of my father. She wasn't in the least interested."

"She wouldn't be," Bing said. "And for once let's be glad that it seemed of no consequence to her. But it may be a tremendous asset to us later on. One never knows; in this game one learns that every card one holds may prove an ace or a joker sooner or later."

He got back into the car having first helped Melina into her seat.

"Now we have got to be absolutely ready with our story," he said as they drove off towards Fez.

"Is anyone likely to question us about it?" Melina inquired.

"You never know," he answered. "You, Melina Lindsay, came out to Tangier with Mrs. Schuster as her secretary because we had had a tiff. We had been married only a short while and after a row I walked out on you—went back to the States. So you reverted to your maiden name and took a job. Fortunately I had a change of heart and arrived just as Mrs. Schuster had sacked you, to carry you off on a second honeymoon. O.K.?"

"It sounds all right," Melina said doubtfully. "I've never been to America, of course."

"Well, I have," he answered. "I lived there for over a year so that part is easy. What we have got to choose is a nice name. What do you fancy? Don't choose anything so difficult that you won't remember it."

"The only American I ever knew well," Melina said reflectively, "was a girl in the office where I learned to type. Her name was Cutter."

"Fine! That will do," Bing said. "Mr. and Mrs. Cutter! Not very distinguished, but then we don't want to be obtrusive, do we?"

Melina was looking ahead down the darkening road and didn't answer him for the moment. And then, as the outline of Fez came in sight against the evening sky, she said: "Bing, I'm frightened!"

"So am I," he answered. "But I keep thinking of that little boy and wondering how frightened he must be."

Melina gave herself a shake. Yet the fears which lay at the back of her mind came crowding in on her as they passed quickly through the French part of the town and now at last she saw the huge walls of the native city.

They passed one gateway into it and then came to another around which was seething an enormous number of people. Now the fluorescent lighting of the modern Fez was left behind and there were flares on the sides of the streets, the lighted windows of tall, ancient houses, and the noise, dust and stench of the Arab quarter.

In any other circumstances Melina would have been thrilled and excited. As it was she stared wide-eyed at the chattering, shouting crowds, at the veiled women, at the men with their turbans, fezes or hooded burnous.

Bing was too intent on driving carefully through the crowds to notice anything but the figures which kept running in front of him, the laden donkeys which blocked his way or the bicycles which refused to let him pass. Dark eyes turned to stare at them, but they were by no means the only tourists to be seen. There were Americans, fat Germans with expensive cameras hung round their necks, Italians joining in the noise and the laughter, Spaniards looking gloomy, and even a number of middle-aged English women who had obviously come on a bus tour accompanied by a courier who pointed out places of interest to them in a strident voice.

The road, with its colourful stalls and shops, seemed endless. Finally it widened and Bing parked the car beside two or three others and permitted a small boy to look after it.

"Come along, honey," he said with a nasal twang. "We've just got to buy a few souvenirs to take home with us."

Melina repressed a desire to giggle at his accent and let him lead her back into the street down which they had driven. There was the smell of mint and onions, the tang of leather, of horses, sheep and goats, and over it all the indescribable, mysterious smell of the East which Melina felt, though she had never smelt it before, was exactly what she had expected.

Figures rushed by them; dark eyes stared at them from behind yashmaks; a big man, shouting angrily,

57

pushed them to one side to allow a herd of bleating lambs to pass.

"It's market day tomorrow," Bing said quietly.

They stopped outside one of the shops and Bing allowed the shopkeeper to show him some native shoes embroidered with gold thread, hesitated over them, turned them over and asked the price, and finally said:

"We can't make up our minds for the moment. We'll come back later."

They crossed the road to do much the same performance in a shop which sold brocades, muslins and cottons, all dyed the brilliant colours of the rainbow and which were exciting the interest of a number of Moslem women.

Then they walked on again and stopped beside a stall covered with cheap jewellery. There were bangles, glass and brass; there were necklaces of multi-coloured paste and dozens of long gilt chains from which hung the Hand of Fatima.

Everyone in the Eastern countries knows the Hand of Fatima which is considered lucky. Nearly every Moslem child wears one round its neck. But Melina had never seen one until now and she stared at them with interest.

"I know you'd like one of those," Bing said, "but these aren't good enough."

He turned to the shopkeeper.

"Have you got a Hand with real stones?" he inquired.

"What stones would you like, Sir?" the shopkeeper asked.

"Rubies, if possible, although, of course, red means danger."

"There is no danger in the Hand of Fatima," the shopkeeper answered. "Only good fortune for you, Sir, and for your lady."

"Of course, I was but joking," Bing said.

"I will see what I can find you, Sir, if you will step inside."

Melina had a quick impression that Bing's questions

and the shopkeeper's replies had a special meaning; and when they crossed into the small, cell-like shop which was piled high with leather goods, carpets and embroidered slippers, her suspicion was confirmed.

"Come this way, Sir, I have something which will be of great interest to you," the shopkeeper was saying. And then swiftly he had pulled aside a hanging carpet and revealed a small door behind it.

Bing went ahead and Melina followed. The other side of the door was in darkness and for a moment she stood there, uncertain and afraid to go forward. Then she felt Bing search for her hand and he was pulling her up a narrow, rickety staircase on to the first floor.

"Open the door at the top, Sir, and you will be able to see your way," she heard the shopkeeper say behind them.

They reached the top, Bing turned the handle of a door and they were stepping into a room lit by an oil lamp on a small table in the centre. There was no furniture, only cushions on the floor, and the window veiled by lace curtains looked out over the crowded, busy street they had just left.

Bing turned and held out his hand to the shopkeeper.

"Did you recognise me, Rasmin, you old rascal?" he asked.

"Not for a moment, Mr. Ward. Your accent deceived me and your glasses. Then, when you spoke, when you made the sign, I was sure it was you."

"You were expecting me?" Bing asked.

"There was a telephone call earlier this afternoon," Rasmin answered.

He indicated the cushions on the floor, then going to the door clapped his hands. A woman appeared, veiled and wearing the shapeless, flowing white robes which made it difficult to tell whether she was young or old.

"Tea for two good customers," Rasmin said to her.

He waited until she had gone and then turned with a smile towards Bing and Melina, who were already seated on the leather cushions.

59

"Your daughter?" Bing asked.

"My niece," Rasmin replied. "My daughter has taken a position in Marrakesh. She might be useful to you."

"Shall we be going there?" Bing inquired meaningly.

"The answer lies in the Hand of Fatima," Rasmin replied.

"You are doing well here?" Bing asked.

For a moment Melina was surprised at his conversational tone and the sudden lack of urgency in the way that he sat, comfortably cross-legged on the cushion, and Rasmin sat down with care opposite him. Then she remembered how her father had said that one could never hurry in the East. It was etiquette to be polite, to drink the tea of friendship and then finally, when a European would be seething with impatience, to come to the point.

"Rasmin is an old friend of mine," Bing said, turning to Melina. "Rasmin, this is my wife."

Rasmin bowed and touched his forehead in salute.

"May good fortune and happiness come to both of you," he said.

The mint tea was brought by the Moslem girl and set down on the table. It was hot and sweet in handle-less cups of beaten brass, and Melina burned her mouth before she remembered to sip it slowly.

Finally, after what seemed to her an interminable time, the courtesies had been observed.

"How much do you know, Rasmin?" Bing asked.

"I learned why you were coming here," he replied.

"The child! Is he here in Fez?"

Rasmin spread out his hands with an eloquent gesture.

"I think so," he answered, "but only Allah can be sure."

"How much is known of this?" Bing asked.

"Those who have taken him know and have made much talk of it with their supporters," Rasmin said.

"That we expected," Bing answered. "Are they surprised that there has been no public statement, no publicity?"

"Very surprised," Rasmin said. "They expected a great outcry, headlines in the papers, police and troops searching everywhere."

"It is the one thing that must be avoided," Bing said.

"I think I understand why," Rasmin nodded.

"How many of them are in Fez?" Bing asked.

Again Rasmin made the wide gesture with his arms.

"Who can count the grains of sand?" he questioned. "And yet there are many, like myself, who are loyal but might be too afraid to say so in such a situation."

"That is what I expected," Bing said. "But they will help if necessary?"

"They will help; those who carry the Hand of Fatima," Rasmin answered.

He drew from the folds of his robe a small object which he held out to Bing on the palm of his hand. Melina leaned forward to look at it curiously. It was the Hand of Fatima she saw, just the same shape as those on sale outside hanging from their cheap chains. But this one was different. It was of bright blue enamel in which were set small rubies surrounded by tiny diamonds.

Bing took it from Rasmin's hand with something like reverence.

"There are only three of these in the whole of Morocco," he said. "Do you trust me with this one?"

"It is not I who give it to you," Rasmin replied.

"That I understand," Bing answered. "But I am grateful, very grateful."

"Do not let it be seen," Rasmin said. "Should they know that you have it your life will be forfeit."

"My life is already forfeit on a number of other counts," Bing smiled. "But I agree with you, this might prove a more serious way of dying."

He slipped his hand inside his shirt and Melina saw that he had a leather belt round his waist. He put the tiny emblem somewhere inside it and buttoned up his shirt again.

61

"Where do you think the child is?" he asked Rasmin.

"That is not known as yet," Rasmin replied. "But I have my suspicions."

"He is here in the native town?"

Rasmin shook his head.

"No, I think he is at the house of Moulay Ibrahim."

"Moulay Ibrahim!" Bing ejaculated. "You mean that he is in this?"

"I do not know for certain," Rasmin answered. "But there is a story which came from Tangier that one of the men who spirited away the boy had a deep scar at the corner of his left eye. There is such a man staying at this moment with Moulay Ibrahim—he arrived yesterday."

"Who is he? What do we know about him?"

"He is a Russian," Rasmin said quietly.

Bing suddenly clapped his clenched fist down on the table making the cups clatter.

"Then it is what I expected all along," he cried. "A Communist plot! I said only a few weeks ago that I felt there was infiltration, that the Communists were busy fomenting trouble—but no one would listen to me."

"My information may be incorrect," Rasmin said. "I am only a poor shopkeeper. How could I know what goes on in the minds of the nobility? But the man is there."

"I understood Moulay Ibrahim has always been thought to be loyal."

"Moulay Ibrahim is a law unto himself," Rasmin said. "He is rich; he has his own tribe; he spends a great deal of time in Europe. Why should he worry about other matters? Unless, maybe, he seeks further power!"

"By God! I believe you have got it!" Bing said. "Moulay Ibrahim wants to rule Morocco!"

He had raised his voice a little in the excitement of the moment. Rasmin put his fingers to his lips.

"Take care," he said. "Even the walls have ears! and

now you have stayed here long enough to have made what purchases are necessary."

"How can I get to see him?" Bing asked.

Rasmin bent towards him.

"There is a party at his house tomorrow night," he said. "A big dance. The son of my brother, who works there, tells me of an orchestra brought from Casablanca, of champagne from France and caviar from Russia."

"I have got to be there," Bing said.

"That is agreed."

"Very well," Bing went on. "I shall need an evening suit—a white Tuxedo—and see that it has the mark of an American tailor in it; and dancing shoes, also marked as if they were from New York."

Rasmin nodded.

"I will tell the hotel that I am expecting further baggage to arrive at the station. You will see it is left there?"

"Everything shall be as you desire," Rasmin said.

"And the invitations?"

"The son of my brother will see to those," Rasmin said. "They lie in great piles in the room of Moulay Ibrahim's secretary. It will be easy to extract two of them."

"That is excellent," Bing said. "And now for tonight. If we are to stay at an hotel, which would be best? I shall need a passport. My wife can use her own as she is English. Give it to me, Melina."

Melina did as she was told, taking her passport out of her handbag and holding it out to him. He took it and slipped it into his pocket.

"Our name is Cutter—Mrs. and Mrs. Cutter," he said to Rasmin.

"An American passport for you," the shopkeeper said reflectively. "I think that will be quite easy."

"How long?" Bing inquired.

"An hour; three-quarters. These things should not be hurried."

"Right," Bing said. "My car is parked in the Square

of the Serpent. Tell your boy to meet us here with the purchases we have made in thirty minutes. There is a café, if I remember rightly, a little further along the street. We will go there and eat."

"You will eat well so long as you do not touch the salads forbidden to Europeans," Rasmin smiled.

"You forget nothing, do you, Rasmin?" Bing said affectionately.

He clapped the older man on the back, then said:

"Look at me! Is there anything wrong?"

Rasmin looked him up and down.

"Your hair," he said at length. "It is a little long and they know that a fair haired man was staying in a certain house in Tangier."

"All right then," Bing said impatiently. "Dye it! But for God's sake use one of the new tints from Europe and not some of your hellish Eastern muck. The last time you dyed my hair it took me months to get rid of the stain at the roots."

"We are more experienced now," Rasmin said. "Come quickly; the time passes."

Bing turned to Melina.

"You will be all right here," he said. "I won't be long, I promise you."

He went from the room with Rasmin and Melina heard the door shut behind them. She sat still on the leather cushion, feeling curiously bereft, strangely lonely.

Could this really be happening? she asked herself. And then knew that she was being carried along like a tidal wave by Bing Ward's exuberance, vitality and strong personality. There was something irresistible about him, she thought, and yet at the same time there was something that frightened her too. It was that something which had shown in his face when he had killed that man—she could never forget it.

"I am afraid of him," she thought, and felt herself shiver. She wondered now, if she had the choice over again when he had offered to engage her, whether she would say no. It had seemed then an exciting adventure; now she was not so sure. There was something sinister about everything they did—the feeling they were being watched and pursued; the feeling that she was unwittingly taking part in a drama which affected the whole country.

Then she thought of her father working year after year for little money and no thanks to stabilise the country, to throw out the worst elements in it. He had loved Morocco. "The Garden of Eden" he had called it more than once, and she knew that whatever happened she could not let him down.

Would he approve of what she was doing? She had a feeling that in this battle he would have been on Bing's side and that he would have wanted her not to be a coward. And yet she knew she was a coward. Yesterday her life had been full of her secretarial work, administering the petty needs of Mrs. Schuster, and now she was involved in danger and death, in intrigue, in a war between people who counted each others' lives as cheap and had only one objective—to win.

Then she remembered the little boy and thought that he and she had something in common. They were both pawns in a big game they could not understand.

She heard a sudden acceleration of the noise outside. The shouts, the chatter and the voices had made a background for their conversation which had seemed almost like strange music. Now there were cheers and instinctively, without thinking, she went to the window.

It was impossible to see through the small, dirty panes and not realising that she was being stupid, she opened one side and peered out. Someone was coming down the narrow street on horseback and being cheered as he came.

He was a big man wearing a white burnous and riding a magnificent black horse. He had a white turban on his head and the long end of it encircled his throat.

He was a middle-aged man, but there was something strong and impressive about him—something which quite obviously appealed to the people who cheered and waved to him as he passed by.

He raised his gloved hand in salute and she saw that following him were two other men, servants or companions, wearing Arab dress and keeping closely behind his horse as if they protected him.

The shouts grew louder and were almost deafening as he passed beneath the window where Melina stood watching. And then, as if something attracted him, he glanced up as he rode by and their eyes met. She felt a little shiver go through her. He might look magnificent astride his horse but there was, too, something sinister about him, she thought, something forceful which seemed to strike at her almost as if he shouted at her as he passed.

It was only a momentary impression and then he had gone by raising his hand to the cheering crowd and she was not certain if she had not imagined it. She stood there watching him go and then suddenly she felt her wrist grasped by a hard hand and someone dragged her away from the window and slammed it to.

"You little fool! Why are you showing yourself?" Bing asked.

His tone was offensive and Melina's chin went up defiantly.

"Are you so stupid that you don't understand that we do not want to draw attention to ourselves?" Bing inquired.

The expression on his face made Melina realise what was at stake.

"I . . . I'm sorry," she faltered. "I did . . . not think it . . . would matter. I heard the noise and . . . and wanted to see what was happening."

"And you saw," he said. "I hope you were suitably impressed."

"Who was he?" Melina asked, knowing the answer before he had told her.

"Moulay Ibrahim," he answered.

"Oh, Bing, I'm sorry!" she cried. "I had no idea that he might be passing. I just wondered what the noise was about. It's . . . it's all so exciting for me."

"Did he see you?" Bing asked sharply.

She would have thought it a strange question if she had not already realised he had an extraordinary intuition in picking up the unexpected. She wanted to lie but she knew she dare not.

"He looked up," she said.

"He did!" Bing said grimly.

He saw the expression on her face and put his hand on her shoulder.

"It's all right," he said. "This is a shop. There's no reason why you, as a tourist, should not be looking out of it. And if you were a tourist you would naturally be intrigued by the noise and excitement and want to know what it was all about."

"I'm sorry," Melina said again. "I'll try to be more sensible and not to do things which might be dangerous."

Intent on what they had been saying to each other she had not taken in Bing's appearance until he stepped a little nearer to the light. Then she saw that his hair had been cut in a different fashion and now it was much darker—not sensationally so, but the fairness had gone and he was a kind of mid-brown, an indescribable shade which nobody would notice and on which no one would make any comment.

"Do you like it?" Bing asked with a smile.

"It changes you," Melina said.

"That is what we hoped it would do," Bing replied. "But it's wet and I can't touch it or put my cap on. However, we can't wait here any longer. Come along, and be ready to tell Rasmin when we get downstairs that his goods are charming."

They negotiated the narrow, rickety stairs—there was a light on them now which made it easier—and slipped back into the shop from behind the hanging carpet. Once there Bing began to talk in a loud voice, flourishing a note-case filled with dollar bills. He had not had those before, Melina thought, and wondered who would reimburse Rasmin for all this expense.

"Will you send a porter to meet me at the car?" Bing said as they reached the door. "And don't let him be late. I shan't be more than twenty minutes and I don't want to hang about in this crowd."

"It shall be as the gentleman desires," Rasmin said in the humble, ingratiating voice of the shopkeeper.

"You have got some mighty fine things here," Bing went on. "I'll tell my friends back home to look you up when they come to Morocco."

"A thousand thanks, Sir. You are indeed gracious," Rasmin smiled.

Melina held out her hand.

"Thank you for letting us see all your lovely things," she said. "I only wish we could buy more of them."

Rasmin just touched her hand and then put his hand to his forehead and his heart. They left him and pushed their way up the crowded street to the café.

Here they sat and Bing ordered a strange dish which he told everyone within hearing had been recommended by a friend of his in New York and which, despite looking rather unpleasant, tasted delicious when it finally appeared. Then there was fruit, goats-milk cheese on freshly-baked bread, and mint tea which was not nearly as pleasant as that which had been served by Rasmin.

Finally, after nearly three-quarters of an hour, Bing paid the bill with a lot of by-play as to not understanding exactly what money was required and how much to leave as a tip. Then they retraced their steps towards the car.

A boy was standing beside it with half-a-dozen packages badly wrapped up in coloured paper. Bing unlocked the door, took the parcels from the boy and chucked them on to the back seat. He gave him half a dollar and took it back again, then changed it for some French francs. He tipped the small child who had looked after the car and then they turned right and continued through the brightly lit streets towards another gate of the town.

"Where are we going?" Melina asked as finally they drove through a high, pointed gate and out into the darkness.

"To an hotel," Bing answered. "My passport will be behind us on the back seat. Lean back and get it, will you?"

She did as she was told, unwrapping the piece of paper to reveal the mid-blue pasticised cover.

Bing brought hers out of his pocket.

"There's just a small amendment on yours," he said.

Melina opened it. She saw the words "married woman" had been added and the name of "Cutter".

"Don't worry," Bing told her; "the additions are written in an ink which only lasts for forty-eight hours. Tomorrow you may have lost your husband one way or another."

"You think of everything," Melina said half sarcastically.

"Don't boast," Bing begged. "It's unlucky."

His words made her remember once again the danger of this seemingly mad adventure. One could never escape from it. It was there, all around them in the darkness, even in the car.

Then in a very small voice she asked a question that had been troubling her ever since they set out from Tangier but to which, until now, she had been too nervous to give expression:

"When we get to the hotel," she said, her voice slightly tremulous, "and we ... we say we are ... married; do we ... I mean can we still ask for ... two single rooms?"

5

There was a gentle knock on the door and Melina, who was only half asleep, was instantly wide awake.

"Who is it?" she asked.

In answer the door at the far end of the bedroom opened softly and she could see Bing's shoulders silhouetted against the light of the room beyond.

"It's eight-thirty," he said apologetically, "and I think if we're going to order breakfast I'd better bring these things back."

"Of course," she agreed. "Wait one moment."

He turned away and she slipped out of bed into her dressing-gown which was lying over a chair. Then she drew back the curtains from the window and the sunshine came flooding in, enveloping her in its golden rays which dazzled her eyes and made her lift up her face towards it like a flower towards the light.

Then her eyes cleared and she saw a vision of high palm trees, climbing bougainvillaea, crimson and pink geraniums and white lilies; and beyond, the sand-coloured walls of the native city of Fez.

The hotel to which Bing had taken her was just outside the walls, high up on a hill, and, he told her, it had once been a palace belonging to a former Sultan. The proprietors had done little to spoil the atmosphere. The rooms were furnished in Moorish fashion. There were coloured tiles on the walls; there were Moorish carvings, hangings which might have come straight from a story of the Arabian Nights, and all the main rooms opened on to a terrace on which was a large and tinkling fountain surrounded by palm trees and flowers.

The night before, when they had arrived, the fountain had been lit with coloured lights and Melina had thought it beautiful. But this morning, in the sunshine, she thought that it had a beauty beyond comparison with anything she had seen before.

She stood there staring until a noise in the room behind her made her turn round. Bing was struggling through the communicating doorway with sheets, blankets and pillows and now he put them down on the empty bed which stood beside Melina's.

"I'll make it," Melina said turning towards him.

"Thank you," he answered. "Making beds is something I have always hated doing ever since I was in my preparatory school and matron said I was the worst bedmaker in the whole dormitory. I've had a complex about it ever since!"

He turned back into the small sitting-room where he had spent the night and Melina, knowing the narrowness of the couch on which he had made his bed, felt somewhat guilty as she tucked in the blankets and then disarranged them again to look as if someone had just got out of bed.

"You're up early," she said.

"We've got a lot to do today," he replied, coming back into the doorway to watch her finish the bed.

It was then that she remembered that she was wearing only a nightgown and dressing-gown and that she had not arranged her hair or powdered her nose since she rose.

"Oh, goodness!" she said in sudden confusion. "Don't look at me. I've forgotten, in the excitement of seeing the view outside the window, what I must look like."

"You look very fresh and young," he said in a tone of voice that somehow did not make it a compliment.

"You make me feel like a beatnik," Melina answered scoldingly.

She crossed the room to the dressing-table and was relieved to see that her hair, because it curled naturally round her forehead and over her small head, did not look unattractive. She ran a comb through it and powdered the tip of her nose.

71

"And now," she asked, "What are the plans for today?"

She saw with almost a feeling of chagrin that he was not listening to her nor, indeed, looking at her. He was staring past her through the open window towards the roofs of the city below them.

It was funny to remember, now, she thought, how apprehensive she had been of staying with him in an hotel. He had made it very easy, demanding a suite as soon as they arrived and paying no attention when the receptionist told him that owing to the influx of tourists and the fact that there was a big dance in the neighbourhood the following night, there was no chance of their being accommodated with anything of the sort.

"I like a sitting-room to myself," Bing had asserted in the nasal accent which somehow seemed to make him sound more rich and important than if he had spoken naturally. "Even if I am on holiday I have business to do and my wife doesn't like my papers cluttered all over the place in her bedroom. Find the Manager."

The Manager appeared and Bing reeled off a list of important Americans who, he said, had recommended him to this particular hotel. Finally, someone had been moved from the room they now occupied and the Manager's private office, which happened to be next door to it, was put at their disposal.

"You can't sleep in there," Melina had said half in a whisper, when finally they were alone in the bedroom together.

"It's a jolly sight better than most of the places I have to sleep in," Bing said with a smile. "And I'm quite used to the floor, it doesn't worry me. I can sleep on anything."

Fortunately, however, there was a small couch in one corner on which Melina suspected the Manager took his *siesta*. It was hard and not very comfortable, but Bing pooh-poohed the idea of moving the mattress from the bedroom on to it, and taking only the sheets and the blankets, assured her he would be all right.

72

They had locked the door as soon as they came into the room and Bing had already warned Melina against talking about anything that mattered except in a very low whisper.

"To say the walls have ears is literally true when you are in any Eastern or Middle Eastern country," he said. "The natives know everything. Nothing is too small to escape their notice, nothing is too insignificant to be remembered and relayed on to someone else."

"I remember my father used to say the same thing," Melina said. "It frightens me at the moment."

"With reason," Bing answered in all seriousness.

Long after he had shut the door between them and for all she knew was sleeping soundly, Melina had lain awake thinking over the events of the day and feeling herself bewildered, fascinated and, at the same time, scared by everything that had occurred in such quick succession. How could she have imagined, when she got up that morning, that she would lose her job—a nice, safe, secure one she had thought—and find herself re-engaged and taking part in an incredible, crazy adventure with implications which even now she found hard to believe.

There were so many things, she thought, that she had wanted to ask Bing, and yet somehow there was something about him which made it difficult to encroach on his reserve or those things which he was quite determined to keep secret.

Melina had always been sensitive towards other people's feelings and now she knew it was impossible to probe too deeply or to try and force his confidence. He was a strange man, she had thought a dozen times during the long drive to Fez, and she thought it again now as she watched him looking out of the window and having, for the moment, apparently forgotten her presence.

"Bing, is anything the matter?"

She asked the question almost apprehensively and then with a little start he turned towards her and a smile flickered over his face.

73

"I am sorry," he said. "I was planning something. Get dressed. I'll order breakfast in our sitting-room. They will expect us to do so as I made such a fuss about having it."

He walked out of the room, closing the communicating door behind him. Melina hurried to have her bath and put on one of her prettiest cotton dresses which she had remembered to ask the maid to press the night before. She arranged her hair, powdered her face and put on a little lipstick. It was already beginning to get hot and she knew that in the heat the less make-up she used the better she would look.

She had hurried, but it was nearly nine o'clock before she opened the door and went into the sitting-room. The waiter, wearing the traditional long, white cotton robe, a spotless, cleverly turned turban, and with bare feet, was bringing in the breakfast—long glasses of fruit juice, eggs with tiny curls of crisp bacon, fresh rolls and butter which looked delicious but which Melina already knew tasted slightly rancid.

"I am just hoping, honey, that the coffee is drinkable," Bing said as she came into the room. "I haven't had a decent cup since we left New York."

"You must learn not to fuss so much about your coffee," Melina said, thinking as she did so that they sounded exactly like a comfortably married couple who had grown used to each other's likes and dislikes.

The waiter left them alone and Melina raised her eyebrows.

"Eggs!" she said. "Isn't it too hot for that?"

"You may not get any lunch," Bing warned her.

She smiled at that and ate her eggs with enjoyment, finding, as she had expected, that the butter was nasty and the jam, made from tiny strawberries found at the foot of the Atlas Mountains, was delicious. The oranges, which had obviously been picked locally, were small and sweet.

They ate in silence for some minutes, then Bing said:

"I have decided the best thing we can do today is to

go and reconnoitre round the house where the party is to be held tonight."

"I was expecting you would say that," Melina answered. "I should like to see where Moulay Ibrahim lives."

"It isn't the sort of place where he ought to live or where he would feel most at home," Bing replied. "He was born in the desert. His father was a small Sheik who, owing to his ambitions, rose to be an important one. He made a great deal of money cattle dealing and also, I am convinced, by slave trading and the smuggling of drugs."

Bing made a gesture of disgust.

"Anyway," he went on, "the old Sheik became so rich that he grew bored with the company of his tribesmen and of his innumerable wives. He went on a trip to Paris taking his eldest son with him. His extravagances there, the parties he gave, his excesses, his vices and his general behaviour are still talked about and have become almost a legend."

"It must have been fun in a way," Melina laughed.

"Dope peddling is a dirty business," Bing answered, "but it pays. The Sheik renewed his efforts when he got home. He also required extra cash for his son's education because he left him behind in Paris. Unfortunately the boy was far too imbued with his father's mentality to learn much that was any good to him. Nevertheless, after a few years he came back to take over the chieftainship from his father who was sinking into premature old age, due mostly to the effects of drink and disease."

Bing paused to drink his coffee.

"Moulay Ibrahim had no intention of ruling as his father had ruled," he continued as Melina did not speak. "He had far greater ambitions and he started to enlarge his tribe in every way he could, to make his possessions larger and even more impressive than those owned by his father, and to do what had never been done by his ancestors before, to cultivate the friendship of the Europeans."

75

Melina had put her elbows on the table and was listening intently. She was seeing, as Bing talked, the commanding figure astride the black horse, his dark, flashing eyes that looked up into hers.

"Moulay Ibrahim didn't only want money, he wanted power," Bing went on. "And he found that one of the first ways to get himself known was to entertain. He built an enormous villa on the foundations of an old palace, which I hope we shall see tonight, outside Fez. He built another in Casablanca and also purchased property in Marrakesh."

Bing's voice altered and became cynical.

"It is never difficult to get people to accept invitations to a superbly organised party," he said. "The French citizens of every town which Moulay Ibrahim patronised were only too willing to dance to the orchestras he had flown from France and enjoy the expensive cabarets which were even sometimes brought from as far as New York."

"I don't blame them for going," Melina said quickly.

"Neither did anybody else," Bing said. " But it was not generosity which made him play host, it was something quite different."

"What was it?" Melina asked, then sat up suddenly, surprised by the expression on Bing's face.

She could see that he was listening, tense and still, with his ears strained. She listened, too, but could hear nothing. Then soundlessly he rose to his feet, walked to the door and jerked it open. The waiter was standing outside very near to the door. If he was surprised he did not show it.

"What do you want?" Bing asked sharply.

"If the gentleman has finished with the breakfast I will take away the tray," the waiter said submissively.

"Yes, we have finished," Bing replied abruptly.

Melina got to her feet so as to allow the waiter access to the table.

"Get your things," Bing said. "We've got a lot of sight-seeing to do. The sooner we start the better. Don't forget the guide book."

76

"No, I won't," Melina replied.

She was aware, as she went to her bedroom, that her heart was beating a little quicker. Had the waiter been listening to what they were saying? And if he had, did it matter? Bing had been speaking in a very low voice, and yet even a low voice might have carried as far as the door. They had been speaking in English, but who was to know whether the waiter could understand English or not? There was no reason why they should not talk of Moulay Ibrahim, and yet, at the same time, it was unlikely that an American would have known so much about him.

As she put a clean handkerchief into her bag she began to feel frightened again. She and Bing were so vulnerable—two English people alone fighting against inconceivable odds and without the slightest knowledge as to who and where their enemy might be or what he would look like should they find him.

"The child! Remember the child!" she told herself fiercely. That was what mattered. It was no use getting frightened, no use getting panicky. It was the child who mattered and it seemed that very soon they might be at the end of their quest.

Her bag was ready and she picked up her sunshade. She had brought only two hats abroad with her, but she hadn't been foolish enough to under-estimate the sun or to imagine, as so many Europeans do, that her hair would be enough protection. She slipped the hook of the sunshade over her arm and remembered that Bing had said, "Bring the guide book". She hadn't got one, but she had in her case a paperbacked novel which she had been reading. She thought she had better carry that and make herself look as much like the usual tourist as possible.

Bing was waiting for her in the sitting-room. They went downstairs, which were of the cool stone of the old Moorish palace, but were highly polished so that Melina held tightly on to the banisters for fear she should slip.

There was a crowd round the reception desk talking

about rooms and excursions and Melina waited while Bing bought two highly coloured postcards of the hotel.

"We mustn't forget to send these home," he said, and demanding loudly two stamps for the United States of America he stuck them on.

"Put these in your bag," he told Melina, "and we'll write them when we're in the Sultan's Palace. That'll give the folks a real thrill."

"I'm sure it will," Melina said, longing to laugh but realising that all this was too serious to be really funny.

Having established his American identity, Bing then walked with Melina through the hotel and out into the courtyard. Their car was parked where they had left it the night before, in a row with a number of other cars. But now, where the courtyard had seemed quiet and deserted in the darkness, it was alive with people, movement and colour.

The hotel servants were busy bringing out the luggage for a bus load of tourists who were leaving for their next beauty spot, with the usual number of twittering, excited ladies carrying guide books and souvenirs, accompanied by tired, rather bored husbands who would much rather have spent their holidays at home working in the garden.

Melina was not really interested in the tourists, but looked beyond them to where, through an arched courtyard, she could see a number of natives peering in at them, apparently trying to excite their attention.

"What do those people want?" she asked Bing.

He glanced towards them as he helped her into the car.

"Oh, they are guides," he said. "At least, the ones in the black and white striped cotton night-shirts are. The others are beggars, fortune-tellers, snake-charmers and Heaven knows what else. They are not allowed in the hotel courtyard, thank goodness, but we've got to run the gauntlet to get through them. Shut your window and leave it to me."

It was really quite an ordeal, Melina thought, as Bing, driving the car very slowly, refused three or four

78

guides in succession, a man who wanted to sell him a raffia hat, another with leather book-markers and a third with children's windmills. Pushing behind them, shouting, waving, screaming their wares, were a large number of other natives and several women with tiny babies who held out their hands and begged for money.

"I feel we ought to give them something," Melina said with a sigh as at last the car was free of the encroaching crowd and they moved away swiftly, blowing up a cloud of dust over those who petitioned them.

"If you give once you have to give again," Bing said. "The word goes round. They know at a glance if you're a sucker, then they never leave you alone. They are professionals. You can't shake off a professional whatever you say to him."

Melina laughed.

"It's all so exactly as I thought it would be," she said. "The beggars, the people selling things, the dust, the palm trees—oh, everything! I think I should be the happiest person in the whole world if it wasn't that we've got to find that child."

"And quickly!" Bing said quietly.

"Suppose we do find him tonight," Melina said. "What are we going to do?"

"I don't know," Bing answered. "It's impossible to make plans. One can only pray that something will turn up at the last moment; that somehow, by some extraordinary and unexpected miracle, one can achieve the impossible."

There was something in his tone which made her look at him quickly.

"You don't think we are going to find him, do you?" she said.

"I don't know," Bing said wearily.

She felt he did not wish to speak of it any more and contented herself in watching the road ahead. They were climbing steadily and now the country was green with trees and the cultivated slopes of the hills, and on the road were white bullocks being led along by a very small child on a donkey, laden with what seemed an

79

almost incredible load of straw and green bushes but which seemed to trot beneath them jauntily and unconcernedly.

"Is this the way to Moulay Ibrahim's house?" Melina asked.

"It's not the direct way to it," Bing answered. "I want, if possible, to get a little above it. I can't remember quite how high up the hill it is."

After a mile or so he turned off the main road on to what was little more than a cart-track winding between great boulders, which looked as if they had been thrown there by some giant, and stunted trees with thick trunks and strange, flat, wide branches.

On they climbed until finally Bing stopped the car under a tree and got out. He opened the door for Melina, then produced two cameras from the back seat.

"One for you and one for me," he said. "We've got to do the thing properly."

"Where did these come from?" Melina said.

"Rasmin provided them with our other purchases," he said. "They are jolly expensive ones, too, so we mustn't forget to return them."

"Who is Rasmin? You must tell me about him," Melina said. "And you haven't finished your story about Moulay Ibrahim."

"It was very foolish to speak as I did," Bing said.

"Do you really think the waiter overheard?"

"I don't know," Bing answered. "But one thing was quite certain—he was trying to. It may have been just routine; all the native servants spy for somebody. If it isn't for the Government or those who are against the Government, or for the police, or for the hotel proprietors, it's for the shopkeepers who want to know how much money the tourists have got and if it's worth their while sending a free gift or something which will attract them to their shops."

He sighed.

"No native boy can resist the excitement, the intrigue, of knowing a little bit more than his friends know, of having some tit-bit of information to impart that somebody else wants."

"I can see it's a kind of game," Melina said.

"It is, unfortunately, something that they as a nation are very good at and we, as reserved, inhibited British, are very bad at," he answered.

He took Melina by the arm and started to lead her up a steep incline through the trees to what was obviously the summit of a little hill. Her feet slipped in the sand and it filled her sandals, making it hard for her to walk; but, finally, with Bing's help, she got to the top. Then she gave a little gasp.

The view was magnificent. It seemed to stretch out on the right to a shimmering, heat-laden horizon where the land merged into the sky. A little to the left of them was the city of Fez with its great high walls, its spires and minarets, its palm trees; and beyond it the white modern buildings of the French quarter.

Just below them, brilliant in the sunshine, glittering, shining almost as if it were a glorious jewel, lay the villa they had come to seek. It was surrounded by a wall, although at first Melina's eyes were only for the glimpses she could see of shining fountains, of dark cypress trees, of great splodges of colour, so vivid, so breathtaking in their loveliness that she felt as if she looked at a picture painted by a master Impressionist who had used every colour on his palette.

The villa itself was enormous. She could see the long, wide rooms with their low parapets; she could see the windows, iridescent in the sunshine, which opened on to the gardens. There were dozens and dozens of them and yet the whole thing was so perfectly proportioned that one felt that it might have been built by some Grecian architect rather than that it belonged to this century.

There was a swimming pool, blue as the Mediterranean as it reflected the sky above it . . . And then, as if her eyes were satiated with so much luxury and beauty, she looked a little closer to what she saw was preoccupying Bing—the wall round the villa.

81

The ancient people who had built the city of Fez had built to keep their enemies out. Moulay Ibrahim had done the same thing. The wall was not so high but it was equally unclimbable. Of local stone, it surrounded the whole villa save for the entrance at the far end where two great iron gates were guarded by sentries.

Though the wall was not abnormally high it was ornamented all along the top with great spikes set at strange angles which would have impaled anyone mad enough to attempt to scale it.

Suddenly the beauty and the colour inside seemed somehow sinister.

"It's . . . it's a prison," Melina whispered almost beneath her breath.

"Moulay Ibrahim's father, who built the wall round the old palace, was reputed to have two hundred wives," Bing answered. "In Fez I was told that they were so lovely that every young man grew up in the native city with the ambition to see at least one of them. The old Sheik made quite certain that there was no chance of their doing that."

"If the child is there," Melina said, "what chance have we got of getting him out?"

"That was just what I was wondering," Bing said.

He threw himself down on the ground and drew from under his shirt a pair of binoculars. They were not very large ones, but Melina felt a memory vaguely stirring in her mind of someone who had talked to her about a German firm who had invented binoculars which were so powerful that miles away one could see a fly on the wall.

"Keep a look round to see that no one is watching us, there's a good girl," Bing said.

She wanted to resent his tone because it was so casual and yet authoritative, but with a mental shake of her shoulders she told herself to remember that he was her employer. If he gave her an order he had every right to do so. But somehow, in that moment, she resented his ceasing to be the charming companion and becoming suddenly aloof and nearly a commanding officer.

Then she knew that this was a Bing she had not seen before; a Bing at work, concentrating to the exclusion of all else, a man dedicated to the task which was on hand. He kept his head down as low as he dared and the binoculars were almost against the ground. It was a wise precaution, Melina thought. Anyone approaching him, except from the front, would imagine he was resting and would have no idea of his real occupation until they were right up to him.

She looked round as he had told her to do. There was nothing in sight except some long-eared goats nibbling at the dry grass and a hawk high overhead, poised, quivering against the sky. She could see Bing was searching every inch of the villa, window by window, door by door. At last her curiosity could be contained no longer.

"Can you see anything?" she asked.

"No," he said, "nothing."

He rose and moved into the shadow of some trees. There was a clump of stones and he crouched behind it, having first looked around to see he was not observed, and lifted the glasses once more to his eyes.

Melina had followed him and now as she watched him inspecting the windows once again she gave a little gasp.

"There's a man—a man in the garden," she whispered.

Bing swung his glasses to the left. There had only been one man when Melina spoke, but now there was another. They were both of them wearing white trousers and open necked shirts. They looked in the distance as if they were Europeans, Melina thought, but it was impossible to judge. Only Bing would know through his powerful glasses.

"Can you see them clearly?" she asked. "Who are they?"

Without a word he handed her the glasses and steadying herself against the rocks she put them to her eyes. They were so strong that she almost gasped when she had them first focussed on the men. It was almost as if she was beside them, talking to them, they were so vivid.

One man was standing looking down at the swimming pool. He was dark and she had the impression that he might be a Moroccan, but she was not sure. The other was undoubtedly fair skinned and yet it was difficult to imagine what nationality he might be.

"If you are looking at the man on the right," Bing said quietly, "do you see anything unusual about him?"

"No . . . I don't think so," Melina said. And then she saw it—a scar running from his left eye down the side of his face!

She gave a gasp and Bing bent over and took the glasses from her.

"Come away," he murmured. "We've seen enough."

"Then the child is there! That is the man who took him," Melina cried.

"Don't waste time talking," Bing said. "I want to get away from here."

"Why?" Melina asked. "You don't think they have seen us?"

"One never knows," Bing answered. "Someone might have noticed the sunshine on the lenses of the binoculars. Someone might be watching to see who visits the hill above the villa. Moulay Ibrahim has sentries at the gates but he also has eyes everywhere."

"But we know the child is there," Melina said, thinking Bing was being unnecessarily panicky when, after all, they had discovered what they wanted to know.

He hurried her so quickly to the car that she had no time to say more. He pushed in the gears and set off down the dusty track towards the main road. They reached it and he turned to the left, away from Fez, and started to drive very swiftly along the smooth, well built road.

"Where are we going?" Melina said. "Oh, please tell me. I'm so excited now that we have discovered the child. Can't we send soldiers or police or something to get him away?"

"If the soldiers battered their way into Moulay Ibrahim's villa," Bing said grimly, "there wouldn't be one chance of their finding anything. Small bodies are very easily disposed of."

"Do you mean they would kill him?" Melina asked in horror.

"I mean that Moulay Ibrahim would never be incriminated by being found with the evidence of the crime," Bing answered. "He is far too cute for that. No, we have got to be far more subtle, far more clever."

"But how?" Melina asked. "How?"

Bing did not answer and she knew that her question irritated him. She relapsed into silence, biting her lips to keep back the stream of questions which longed to be asked but to which she knew, in all justice, there was no answer.

Bing drove on and on, then turned and dropped down from the mountains a little. There was a small village below them lying, Melina guessed, on the very outskirts of the suburbs of Fez; not really a part of the city but somehow having got joined to it by the encroaching growth of the population.

"Will there be a telephone there, do you think?" Melina asked, knowing instinctively why Bing was thinking of stopping.

"Look back over your shoulder," he said. "Is there a yellow car following us?"

She glanced back.

"Yes," she said. "There is a car and it's yellow."

Bing suddenly slowed down his speed.

"It was outside the hotel when we left this morning," he said.

"You mean it might be someone following us?" Melina asked in a kind of horror.

"It's a chance we've got to consider," he answered. "We are tourists! Think now—where would tourists want to go? And what would they do on this particular road?"

Melina pointed below them to where, in a field, two white oxen were pulling a primitive native cart which was being filled with some sort of crop by two women.

"I think that tourists would want to photograph that," she said.

"Of course," Bing answered. "Thank you, Melina."

He drew up on the roadside.

"Don't look round," he said. "Just be intent on focussing your camera."

She watched him as he brought a light indicator out of his pocket and considered it absorbedly. She heard the car approaching them and it was with the greatest effort she did not look round. Instead she moved first this way and then another trying to get the oxen in focus. The women working in the fields suddenly saw them and screamed a Moslem protest of modesty and indignation. Bing bowed to them and threw several coins spinning through the air which they scrawled for eagerly.

Now at last they could turn away. The yellow car was out of sight.

"Perhaps it was all right," Bing said a little uncertainly but not, Melina thought, very hopefully.

They got back into their own car and drove down the road.

"I don't think it would be safe to telephone anywhere near here," Melina said. "It is what they would expect you to do."

"You're right, of course," Bing said. "You are quite right. I must not go near a telephone, but somehow I have got to get a message to my friend. It will be something for him to know where his boy is, if nothing else."

"Couldn't Rasmin do it?"

"Of course! Of course he could!" Bing said. "We will go back and complain about some of the goods we bought yesterday. Reach back and see what they are."

Melina did as she was told. The parcels were still where they had put them last night and she opened the first one to find a pair of leather shoes with wooden soles.

"We will say they hurt your feet and we want to change them for something else," Bing said. "I'll make quite a fuss about it. That ought to sound convincing."

At the next crossroads he turned the car to the right, going back towards the native town. Then he put out his hand and laid it on Melina's.

"Thank you," he said, "for helping me. Somehow I didn't expect you would."

She felt annoyed at his words.

"What do you mean by that?" she asked.

"What I said," he answered. "I never imagined a girl could be as helpful as you have been. You were so quick the time I jumped on to the balcony. I was hoping, almost against hope, there might be a man there—an Englishman. I felt he might understand. But you couldn't have been better. And now, despite all my misgivings, I'm glad you're with me."

"You seem to have a very poor opinion of the female sex," Melina said.

For a moment there was silence then Bing took his hand away and put it back on the wheel.

"I suppose that is the truth," he said. "Perhaps I've met the wrong sort of women—as my mother would have said had she been alive."

"Have they made you cynical or bitter? Melina asked.

"Both," Bing answered.

There was a note in his voice which made her think that somehow she had struck him on the raw.

"What happened?" she asked curiously. "Did you love somebody very much and then they behaved badly to you?"

To her astonishment Bing hit the wheel with the palm of his hand with a sudden vicious blow which made her feel that he would have liked to have hit her.

"Be quiet!" he shouted. "Don't poke and probe. It's what all women do. You're all the same; every one of your sex. You want to get a man under a microscope as

87

if he was a moth impaled on a pin, and then you start to dissect him. 'Why do you think this?' 'Why do you do that?' Shut up, damn you! Let my life be private and let me have some secrets which are my own."

Melina sat absolutely still, tense with astonishment. She had never been spoken to, in her whole life, so rudely and so offensively. And yet, at the same time, she knew that underneath Bing's anger there was pain—real pain and unhappiness. Some woman, she thought, had got him very much on the raw.

6

Melina looked at herself in the mirror and wondered if she was smart enough for such an important party. To her own eyes her dress of turquoise-shaded nylon made her look very young and unsophisticated.

She had brushed her hair until it gleamed with golden lights and she had made up her face very carefully, adding a touch of eye-shadow which she hoped would make her look exotic and exciting. But instead it only seemed to accentuate the blueness of her wide eyes and make her appear younger than ever.

Her only ornament was a necklace of pearls and moonstones which had belonged to her mother. It was an antique necklace which had come from Burma and whenever she wore it she felt as if it brought her luck and that her evening would be a happy one.

She thought now as she slipped on the necklace that she was wishing for safety and a lack of danger more than anything else, but it certainly added to her appearance and she noted, with a little touch of vanity, that her skin looked very white and clear—almost transparent.

She wondered wistfully whether Bing would notice her appearance. He was so intent on his job and his search for the child that she felt he would hardly notice or care if she appeared dressed in a sack; and she could not forget, either, his strange outburst that afternoon when she had questioned him.

After his voice had rung out in protest and anger there had been a long, barren silence while Melina looked out of the window, feeling her cheeks burning crimson because he had spoken in such a way and also because she reproached herself for having seemed curious and prying.

Then about three minutes later Bing spoke.

"I'm sorry," he said in his quiet, ordinary tone. He had then gone on to talk of quite trivial, ordinary things, and she realised, thankfully, that his anger was past and he was striving to make things between them as normal and pleasant as they had been before.

Nevertheless she was well aware that it was a danger signal. Bing was not going to allow her to encroach on his private life and she felt a little resentful that she had been so open in her confidences to him.

During the long drive between Tangier and Fez she had spoken of the loneliness of her life in London and how, after her father's death, she had longed for adventure and to get away from it all.

"I expect he was bored listening to me," she told herself now. And yet even the uncomfortable feeling that she had been over-exuberant and too confiding could not overshadow the little flicker of excitement within herself for what lay ahead this evening.

She had so seldom been to a really big party—in fact all the parties in her life had been few and far between and most of them not worth remembering. The people in the village where she had lived as a child, when she returned there for a week-end, would say:

"Fancy you living in London, Miss Melina! You must find us very dull and stodgy after all your smart parties."

Melina knew it was no use trying to tell them that nearly always when her work was done she would go home to her tiny bedroom at the top of a tall house in Bloomsbury and sit there reading until it was time for bed. Sometimes, as a treat, she would eat at Lyons Corner House, or one of the cheaper restaurants, so as to watch the people. But she had few friends in London and most of those, being of her father's generation, were not the sort to press invitations upon a young girl who they thought was too gay for them.

It seemed absurd that she could not make friends of

90

her own age in the office, but the place where she worked employed nearly all men and most of them had been there thirty years or more. One or two of the younger ones had asked her out from time to time, but they were married men and she refused them with such positiveness that they did not venture to invite her a second time.

No, tonight would be a red letter occasion as far as she was concerned and suddenly, as she looked at herself in the mirror, she threw away her apprehensions and made up her mind to enjoy it.

"When I go back to London it will be something to remember," she whispered to herself. "I shall have seen one of the most beautiful houses in Morocco; I shall have been the guest—though uninvited—of one of the most powerful and dangerous men in the country."

It sounded rather like a film, she thought, and the only thing that was lacking was the love interest. She was not going to find fault with anything, however; and conscious that she looked her best, she opened the communicating door and stood there waiting with sparkling eyes for Bing's approval.

He was putting the finishing touches to his hair which he had brushed upwards in the American manner, and this, with its new darker colour, completely altered his appearance. He put down his hair brush and smiled at her.

"Well, you look real dandy!" he said in exaggerated tones, and she laughed.

"All I can say to you is that you look very American," she retorted.

His tuxedo, with its padded shoulders, was white, and there was no possible doubt that the tailor who had cut it lived in the United States.

As Bing slipped a handkerchief into his breast pocket and picked up his loose money from the chest of drawers, Melina looked round the room and saw that the desk, which had been pushed to one side to make room for a table and comfortable chairs, was now piled high with papers. She looked at them quizzically raising

91

her eyebrows and in a low voice, which he used when he did not wish to be overheard by anyone listening outside the door, Bing whispered:

"My papers! They are all on the American stock market and are quite incomprehensible to me—as I hope they are to anyone else who tries to read them."

"Every detail is of importance, of course," Melina said, speaking seriously but with a teasing note in her voice.

"One day I will explain to you that detail means the difference between success and failure," Bing replied.

He straightened his narrow bow-tie, slipped a large gold ring on to his engagement finger, and held his hand out to Melina.

"What do you think of that?" he asked. "Twenty carat and bought in one of the best jewellers on Fifth Avenue. Haven't you forgotten anything?"

Melina gave a little gasp.

"A wedding ring!" she exclaimed.

"Exactly," Bing answered. "Rasmin thought of it, so I don't take any credit. Try one of these for size."

He pulled an envelope out of his pocket and emptied the contents on the palm of his hand. There were three narrow gold wedding rings and Melina took the smallest.

"I guessed that was the one," Bing said. "And now I'd better hide these. Anyone finding them in my baggage would imagine I'm a bigamist."

She saw him slip the little envelope into a carton of cigarettes which he then threw into a drawer.

"Is that a safe place?" Melina asked.

"Far safer than locking anything up," he answered. "The implication, if one has something locked, is that one doesn't wish anyone to see it—which makes those who are curious 'curiouser and curiouser', as the White Rabbit said."

"I only hope that I will remember that my name is Cutter," Melina answered. "That is the most difficult thing for me to learn at the moment. Are you ready?"

"I am ready," Bing said solemnly, "if you are."

She picked up her evening scarf, which was of white silk with a fringe at either end, and carrying only a small evening bag which contained her handkerchief and her vanity case she walked across the floor in front of Bing, thinking that the stiletto heels of her silver shoes made a noise like the overture at a theatre before the curtain rises.

Bing picked up the invitation which was lying on the table and slipped it into his pocket. They had both studied it carefully before they went to dress. Moulay Ibrahim had invited his guests for seven-thirty which meant, Bing said, that there was going to be so much food and drink it was quite unnecessary to have dinner before they went.

"I expect there will be dancing," he said, "but that will really be for the Europeans. To the Moroccans a party means a good blow-out. I expect the dishes will be mostly European tonight. No roasted sheep and the principal guest being handed the eye as a special titbit! Nevertheless, there will be plenty of it and too much drink anyway, so be prepared for an orgy."

"I'm longing to try real Arab dishes," Melina said.

"Well, I doubt if you will get them tonight," Bing answered. "But, anyway, there are certain to be several things that you have never tasted before."

Melina remembered the conversation as they went down the shining stone stairs to the ground floor. She was feeling quite hungry, she thought, and only hoped her fear that they might be denounced as gate-crashers would not take away her appetite at the last moment.

They drove slowly out of the courtyard and up the hill in Bing's car and almost immediately found themselves in a long queue of other cars all converging towards Moulay Ibrahim's villa.

"There's going to be a good scrum," Bing said with satisfaction, "in which case nobody is likely to notice us, so don't get nervous."

"Supposing he says, 'I don't remember inviting you'," Melina said.

"Even if he thought such a thing, nobody in this

93

country would be so rude as to question our credentials," Bing said. "Once inside the gates we become honoured guests, invited or not. Their rules of hospitality are very strict."

"I remember my father telling me about them," Melina said, "and how even an enemy, once he sits down to eat, must be treated with courtesy and consideration."

"That is right," Bing answered. "Look! There's someone important arriving."

A huge limousine came out of the queue and passed them on the left hand side of the road, speeding up towards the gates.

"Who do you think that is?" Melina asked.

"I have an idea that I have seen the gentleman inside before," Bing answered. "If I'm not mistaken he comes from Russia and is someone I was quite certain would be here tonight."

They drove on and finally came to the gates where an officer in uniform took the invitation which Bing held out to him and told them where he could park the car.

It was all beautifully arranged, Melina thought, as they walked across the green lawns towards the house. There were fairy-lights everywhere which seemed only to echo the stars which were already beginning to twinkle above them although it was not yet dark.

Guests in a long stream were surging up the steps through the tall, white columned entrance and for a moment Bing and Melina stood at the end of a queue which was moving forward step by step. Then Melina felt a pull on her arm and Bing was leading her away across the lawns in the direction of a long balustrade covered with roses.

"Where are we going?" she asked.

"Walk casually," he answered. "We're looking at the flowers and the fountain."

She stopped at the touch of his hand and stared at the fountain which stood between them and the roses. After a few seconds they moved on again and she realised that they were looking over a balustrade into another and lower part of the garden into which, from another flight of steps, guests were descending having obviously passed through the house, been greeted by their host and then returned to the garden again.

This lower garden, Melina thought, had not been visible from the hillside which she and Bing had inspected through the glasses. It was obviously here that the party was to be held.

There was a dance floor built in the centre of it beneath great arches of flowers and lights. There were fountains lit with every colour in the rainbow and floodlights revealed flowers so exotic and so beautiful that some of them could have been arranged or planted only for that particular evening.

At the far end of the garden there was a long buffet laden with food, and already turbaned waiters were passing amongst the guests with trays containing tumblers of whisky and glasses of champagne.

"I think," Bing said, "there is no need for us to be welcomed by our host. We'll skip the preliminaries and join those below us."

"How did you guess that we could do this?" Melina asked.

"I thought when we looked this morning that there were very few preparations for a dance in this part of the garden," he answered. "Therefore, there must be another one somewhere. Q.E.D."

"I suppose I was expecting they would dance in the house," Melina said.

"Much too hot," Bing replied. "But somehow we've got to get into the house later."

There was no need for him to say more. Melina remembered, with a little dropping of her heart, the real reason why they were here. The child! Where would they have hidden him? And she felt guilty and ashamed because she had thought of herself early in the evening rather than of what was happening to the little boy.

She longed to ask Bing how they could get into the

house or, rather, how they could get upstairs. It would be easy enough to wander into the reception rooms; but she was quite certain that Moulay Ibrahim would have an effective guard in the part of the villa he did not wish his guests to penetrate.

She realised, however, that it would be not only silly but dangerous to question Bing at the moment and so she walked silently by his side as they moved forward until they found a flight of marble steps leading into the garden below.

The chatter and noise of voices was rising every moment as more and more guests poured from the house on to the lawns. The orchestra was playing a sentimental foxtrot and quite a number of couples were dancing to it. They were nearly all Europeans, Melina noticed, and felt a sudden pang of envy that some of the women's dresses were glittering with embroidery so that they seemed to reflect the lights and shimmer almost like the water falling from the fountains.

"I feel rather a plain Jane . . ." she began to say to Bing, and then suddenly she caught sight of a woman who had just come into the garden and who was wearing a dress of white net embroidered all over with tiny, sparkling diamante. It was a dress that Melina had seen before.

As she recognised it she gave a litle gasp and clutched at Bing's arm. He stopped dead at the insistence of her fingers and looked towards her inquiringly.

"It is awful!" Melina told him in a quick frightened whisper. "Mrs. Schuster is here! She's standing over there. What are we to do?"

"Nothing," Bing said quickly. "Just act naturally. We can't leave and it will be impossible, even in this crowd, to avoid someone for the entire evening. You've got to face her and we had much better do it at once in case she sees you later when it might prove awkward."

He put his hand over hers as if to calm her and went on:

"Walk up to her and explain that the reason you left

96

Tangier without saying good-bye was because your husband turned up unexpectedly."

"I would not have said good-bye to her anyway," Melina replied bitterly, remembering Mrs. Schuster's unjustified accusation that she was both inefficient and impertinent.

"Never mind! Never mind!" Bing said impatiently. "Whether you've had a row with her or not, it can't matter now. What does matter is the fact that you have got to establish yourself as my wife. To have her rushing round telling everyone that you're really Miss Lindsay might cause complications. Where is she? Just walk across to her naturally."

With an effort Melina pulled herself together. What did it matter what Mrs. Schuster thought? she asked herself. There was more at stake than that spoilt rich woman had ever dreamed in her selfish, empty head. Melina smiled at Bing and lifted her little chin.

"Very well," she said. "I'll try not to let you down— but I can't say that I am going to enjoy it."

Quite a number of people had come between them and Mrs. Schuster since Melina had first seen her. Now with Bing pulling her she pushed her way through to where she had last seen that glittering, lovely gown which she had thought, when she last saw it hanging in Mrs. Schuster's wardrobe, was the most beautiful dress she had ever seen in her life.

Mrs. Schuster had her back towards them as they approached. Melina could see that she was wearing her diamond necklace and the big diamond ear-rings which were shaped like bunches of flowers. She was talking to Ambrose Wheatley, but after one glance towards him Melina did not look at him again.

She reached Mrs. Schuster's side and said in tones that were almost aggressive because she was so nervous:

"Hello, Mrs. Schuster! What a surprise seeing you here."

Lileth Schuster turned round sharply.

"Miss Lindsay!" she exclaimed. And then as if to make certain that her former secretary was really there she repeated: "Melina Lindsay! You're the last person I expected to see. What are you doing here?"

"We've just arrived," Melina replied, and added quickly: "I wanted to apologise for hurrying away from Tangier without saying good-bye. As a matter of fact my husband arrived unexpectedly. I'm afraid I didn't tell you about him, but we . . . we had quarrelled and now we've made it up again."

It all sounded rather breathless and incoherent and Mrs. Schuster raised her eyes from Melina's flushed face and turned towards Bing.

"Your husband!" she exclaimed.

"Yes," Melina answered. "May I introduce him?"

She was unable, however, to complete the sentence. She found herself staring with fascinated eyes at the transformation which suddenly seemed to take place in Mrs. Schuster's face. Her eyes widened, her mouth dropped open and then, with a little cry, she put out both her hands and said breathlessly:

"Bing! It is Bing, isn't it? For a moment I wasn't certain. Oh, Bing! Where have you been? And what have you done to your face?"

Bing's face was impassive but then, as Melina thought afterwards, there had been a second or so for him to recognise Mrs. Schuster before she looked towards him. And yet Melina thought he somehow looked white under his tan as he replied:

"Hello, Lileth! This is, indeed, a surprise."

"Bing, where have you been?" Mrs. Schuster asked softly in a manner which made Melina feel as if she had been eavesdropping. "When I was in London I tried to find you everywhere, but nobody knew where you'd gone."

"I expect I was in the States," Bing answered.

"In the States!" Mrs. Schuster said as if it was Timbuctoo.

"I've had a lot to do out there, as a matter of fact," Bing replied. "It's a long story, but I've had to change my name and so if you were asking for me by my old one it was not surprising you couldn't find me."

"Changed your name!" Lileth Schuster repeated almost stupidly.

"Yes," Bing answered. My Godfather died. He left me some rather useful oil wells on condition that I took his name. It's Cutter now, by the way. You must try and remember it, Lileth—it is spelt in the usual way."

"Oil wells!" Lileth Schuster echoed in almost strangled tones.

Bing was acting the part so well, Melina thought, that she, herself, almost believed in the oil wells and a Godfather called Cutter.

"You've got to tell me about it! I've got to know what it's all about," Mrs. Schuster said and her voice was somehow desperate.

She looked around almost as if she expected an oasis where they could be alone to appear before them. Then seeing the crowds getting larger every moment she said quickly:

"Let's dance, Bing. Ambrose will look after . . ." she paused before she added, ". . . Melina," and Melina had the feeling that she could not bear to say the words, "your wife."

"Very well, we'll dance," Bing agreed. "You will be all right, won't you, Melina? We'll meet by the fountain over there after this dance."

"Melina will be quite all right with me," Ambrose Wheatley intervened, speaking for the first time.

Mrs. Schuster drew Bing away and Ambrose took Melina's hand and guided her on to the dance floor. She moved automatically, too bemused by what had just happened to know what to think.

"Well, really," Ambrose was saying in an almost peevish voice, "you might have told me you were married. It was rather unkind to let me make a fool of myself over you."

"Did you do that?" Melina asked.

She was watching, over his shoulder, Bing dancing with Lileth Schuster. He danced surprisingly well, she thought. She had not imagined he would. And Mrs.

99

Schuster was gazing up into his eyes, her lovely head thrown back, her red lips parted.

Melina forced herself to listen to what Ambrose Wheatley was saying.

"As a matter of fact," he went on, "I was going to find you and apologise for having upset you with my suggestions. I didn't think, somehow, you'd take it like that. It's only that I'm under such an obligation to Lileth. As you know, she's financing my Art Gallery so I don't want to offend her at this particular moment—and she's very, very possessive."

"There was no need for you to apologise," Melina said.

"There was," he insisted. "I realised I said the wrong thing. Instead I was going to ask you to marry me."

Melina dropped her eyes. How easy to say that now, she thought, when he had learnt that she was married and that her husband was with her. She was quite certain that Ambrose Wheatley was far too ambitious and self-seeking to tie himself up to a poverty stricken, unimportant girl however much in love he might be.

"I love you, Melina!" he went on. "I love you and I can think of nothing else. In fact I couldn't sleep last night for thinking of you."

"You mustn't have any sleepless nights about me," Melina smiled. "I don't think my husband would like it."

"Fancy Bing Ward turning up like this—and being your husband," Ambrose said. "I've heard so much about him from Lileth, I feel almost as if I know him. She always described him as being very fair though—he doesn't look very fair to me."

"I think people's hair darkens as they get older," Melina explained rather lamely.

"Well, Lileth won't be pleased he's married to some-body else," Ambrose said reflectively.

"Why? Does she look upon him as her particular property?" Melina asked.

"I should say so," Ambrose answered. "They were engaged to be married at one time."

Melina suddenly felt she could bear to hear no more. This was Bing's story. If he wanted to tell her he would do so. Perhaps this was the reason why he had shouted at her that afternoon, why he had thumped his hand down on the steering wheel. She didn't want to pry things out behind his back.

"It's too hot to dance any more," she said. "Let's go and stand by the fountain."

Ambrose negotiated his way with difficulty towards the end of the dance floor, but as they reached it the music stopped and the dancers poured on to the lawns and towards the buffet, which Melina could now see was heaped with food of every description. They reached the fountain and there was no sign of Bing or of Mrs. Schuster and by now the dance floor was empty.

"I expect they've got a lot to say to each other," Ambrose said, seeing her looking round anxiously. "Come for a walk with me, Melina. I want to talk to you. You're looking very lovely tonight. I don't think you listened just now when I told you that I loved you."

Melina realised suddenly that she hated him.

"I wonder if you would get me a glass of champagne?" she asked. "I haven't had one yet."

"That will be easy," Ambrose answered. "Stay here and I'll get hold of a waiter."

He turned away and he hadn't gone more than a few paces before Melina slipped away into the crowds. She hurried across the lawns until she found herself in the shadows of some trees and bushes which were covered with coloured fairy-lights which looked like glittering jewels.

Here the crowds were not so dense and after a moment Melina managed to find a quiet seat in the shade where nobody would see that she was alone. There she sat for a moment trying to compose her thoughts and to realise the quite fantastic coincidence by which Bing was connected with Lileth Schuster.

How could he have liked anyone like that? she thought—hard, brittle and mean to everyone with whom she came in contact. But in fairness she had to admit that Mrs. Schuster was very lovely, with her great dark eyes, her pointed chin which completed the perfect oval of her face, her beautifully symmetrical figure and the small slim feet which seemed characteristic of every American.

Was that Bing's taste? Melina wondered and was somehow disappointed, though why she did not know.

"Let us sit here, darling!"

It was Mrs. Schuster's voice directly behind her and Melina started.

"We've got to go back. I have to find Melina."

That was Bing speaking and Melina realised now that there was only a hedge of roses and honeysuckle between them.

"Bing darling, darling Bing, why did you leave me? Why did you just disappear like that without telling me where you were going?"

"You told me you were going to marry a man called Fulton—remember?" Bing answered.

"I had to," Lileth Schuster replied. "But I never loved him, you knew that. I loved you."

"You wanted his money and you got it; wasn't that enough?" Bing asked in a hard, aggressive voice.

"Don't speak to me like that," Lileth begged. "You don't know what I went through. Oh, I was rich—rich enough to make any woman happy, I thought. I was wrong. It was agony; worse than that, it was torture being married to a senile old man. I thought money could make up for love, but I was wrong, Bing. I knew when it was too late that I only wanted you, however poor we might be."

There was a silence and Melina wondered what Bing's face looked like. Had he squared his jaw? she wondered. And were his eyes angry or dark with suffering?

"When he died," Lileth went on suddenly, "I tried to find you. I asked everyone we had both known in New York, but nobody had seen you. I was so unhappy I let myself be talked into marrying Carl Schuster. He was an incredible drunk. Our marriage lasted two months then I got a divorce. I came to England. I couldn't find anyone who knew where you were. I wrote to you— not one letter but dozens, Bing—but they were all returned."

"I told you that you couldn't have both money and me," Bing said.

"But now . . . now when you are rich, I . . . I could have had . . . both," Lileth muttered in a strangled voice.

"It's too late," Bing replied. "You forget I'm married."

"To Melina! That milk-faced, stupid little thing. Do you think she will be able to hold you?" Lileth asked scornfully. "You'll be tired of her in a few weeks. She has worked for me and I can tell you . . ."

Melina got suddenly to her feet. She could not sit here, she felt, and let this woman run her down. She could not bear to have all her faults relayed to the man for whom she was now working, the man to whom she was supposed to be married.

Without considering, without thinking of what she was doing, she cried aloud:

"Bing! Bing! Are you there?"

And even as she spoke his name she realised that more than she had ever wanted anything in her life before, she wanted him to come to her.

7

Having called Bing's name, Melina held her breath. Would he come or would he ignore her?

It seemed almost an eternity before he replied:

"Hello, Melina! Where are you?"

"I'm here, behind this hedge of roses," she answered.

"Stay where you are," he replied, "and I'll come round."

She despised herself for eavesdropping, but she could not help drawing nearer the dividing hedge to hear Lileth Schuster say in a low but urgent whisper:

"You can't, Bing. I want to talk to you! I've got to talk to you! There's so much we have to discuss."

"Some other time."

Bing's voice seemed to Melina to be indifferent as if his thoughts were concentrated somewhere else.

"No, no, now, tonight," Lileth insisted. "I haven't seen you for so long. There's so much we have to tell each other. Besides, there's the future to plan."

"Lileth, don't kid yourself," Melina heard Bing say almost sternly. "And now I must go."

"No, Bing! No!"

It was the cry of a spoilt and thwarted woman, but obviously Bing ignored it because there was silence and Melina, knowing Mrs. Schuster, could imagine her sitting there and tapping her long, lacquered nails angrily against the stone seat. It was a habit she had when she was annoyed, and even through the roses and the honeysuckle Melina could sense the rising tempest of her frustration at Bing's departure.

She moved a little away from the seat on which she had been sitting and stood watching the crowds milling around until, at last, she saw Bing coming towards her.

He was walking very slowly and she guessed it was a deliberate effort in order not to call attention to himself.

She could not help a little leap of her heart because he looked so cool, unruffled and so entirely at ease. No one looking at him, she thought, could guess how much was at stake. He came up to her, linked his arm in hers and drew her towards another part of the garden to where there was less light and not so many people.

"Where are we going?" Melina asked after they had walked in silence for a little while and there was, as far as she could see, no one within earshot.

She longed to ask him about Lileth Schuster but she felt it might provoke an outburst from him. Besides, she told herself severely, it was, indeed, none of her business.

"We have got to make a plan," Bing answered.

He stopped in the shadow of a banyan tree in which the fairy-lights had been arranged like flowers amongst the shimmering green leaves.

"We are at the back of the house now," he said casually and not as if he was really interested. "Do you see that wing sticking out to the left? That is where I am sure the boy will be hidden."

"He will be guarded?" Melina asked.

Bing nodded.

"Of course he will."

"Surely it was an extraordinary idea to bring him here and then have a party of this sort?"

"I think the party was planned some time ago," Bing replied. "But apart from that, can't you see that everyone would say exactly what you have done? The boy couldn't be hidden in the house under such circumstances. What is more, that party is a perfect cover to explain the presence of a number of gentlemen of unpleasant antecedents—especially the man with the scar."

Melina nodded.

"Now, what I suggest is this," Bing went on. "We will move about amongst the guests, dancing, eating, seeming to be enjoying ourselves enormously—just in case

105

there's anyone watching us. Then in about an hour's time you will put your hand to your forehead and tell me you think the heat is rather overpowering. I shall take you into the house and hope that by some lucky chance we can get upstairs. While you're fainting I will go and look for something or somebody to help you."

"It sounds too simple to be possible," Melina said.

"When you have been in this game as long as I have," Bing answered, "it is always the simple things that pay off. People expect complications. They are very seldom prepared for a direct attack or something so obviously fundamental as walking through the main gate."

"Bing, supposing ... supposing they catch you," Melina said in a quick whisper. "Wouldn't it be very dangerous?"

Instinctively she put out her hand and laid it on his arm. He looked down at the small, anxious face raised to his.

"Of course not," he answered soothingly. "Don't you know that American citizens are sacred everywhere? I have my passport in my pocket."

He was trying to laugh her out of her fears. And because she felt there was nothing she could say she laughed a little shakily and followed him back over the lawns towards the dance floor.

They danced together and as she had noticed when he was partnering Mrs. Schuster, he was an excellent dancer, light on his feet and with a perfect sense of rhythm. They talked very little for, indeed, there was nothing to say and it was far too dangerous, with so many people round them, to voice anything but the commonplace.

"Come and have something to eat," Bing suggested as the dance ended and he led her across the garden towards the buffet.

Melina had a few sips of champagne but she felt as if food must choke her. She was tense and apprehensive of what lay ahead. She envied Bing and the calm with which he devoured several portions of caviar and a large plateful of langoustines which he told Melina must have been brought from the coast that very morning.

While they were standing there, Melina heard in the distance the sounds of a different sort of music—a strange oriental rhythm which seemed to evoke long-forgotten memories and awaken hidden desires.

"What is that?" she asked.

"Let's go and find out," Bing suggested.

In another part of the garden they discovered an oriental orchestra playing against a specially prepared background of exotic tropical plants and trees in which great snakes and reptiles were half concealed. Melina gave a little cry at the sight of them.

"They are only pretence," Bing said quickly, "Don't be nervous. Moulay Ibrahim will take very good care that none of his guests are harmed tonight; he would lose face if they were."

"But they look almost as if they are moving," Melina said.

"It's a trick of the lighting," Bing replied. "Tinsel paper in front of the bulbs make the snakes' skins shimmer as if they are breathing."

Melina gave a little shiver.

"It's rather creepy," she said, "and somehow the music frightens me. I have longed all my life to hear oriental music, but now it makes me feel strange. I can't exactly explain myself."

"I know what you mean," Bing said. "That is what it's meant to do. See the result."

He made a litle gesture with his hand and she saw that all round in the shadows couples were embracing each other passionately while others were wending their way into the darker, unlit parts of the garden.

"Let's go away," Melina said.

She didn't know why, but she felt Moulay Ibrahim had some particular reason for creating this sort of atmosphere. There was something wrong about it, something vaguely unpleasant. She wished to have no part in it.

"Come back and dance," Bing suggested with a smile, and they were on the floor again, foxtrotting to a tune which had been the rage of London the year before.

"Is this more simple and uncomplicated?" he asked.

"We might even be at a Hunt Ball," Melina replied.

They danced for a long time, so long in fact that Melina did really begin to feel a little weary and hot. There was no wind and the crowds seemed to press in on her so that it was with a quite genuine note in her voice that she said:

"I feel . . . a little overcome with the . . . heat. Could we sit down somewhere?"

She saw Bing's eyes flicker towards his watch and she knew he was wondering if it was too soon to do what they had decided before in a voice of concern he said quickly:

"I'm so sorry honey, you've had a long day one way or another. Let's go and find somewhere comfortable to sit down. I can get you a drink, or perhaps you'd rather have an aspirin?"

"An aspirin would be wonderful," Melina said. "My head is aching rather a lot."

"Let's go indoors," Bing said. "If the air conditioning is on, it will be cooler there."

He put his hand under her elbow and escorted her across the lawn and up the wide, white steps which led to the side door of the villa. There were quite a lot of people going in and out of the house and as soon as they reached the flower-filled veranda off which most of the rooms appeared to open it was obvious that Moulay Ibrahim's guests were taking every opportunity of inspecting his villa.

It was more of a palace than anything else, Melina thought. It had been built on European design, but there were traces of Moorish influence in the coloured tiles, the exquisite hangings and the manner in which quite unexpectedly there was a courtyard with a fountain in the centre of the house.

They moved slowly through the reception rooms,

inspected the courtyard, which was filled with exotic plants, and looked up to where several stories of the house with tiny shuttered and unlighted windows stretched towards the sky.

Melina was well aware that all the time Bing was veering a little to the left, edging towards the wing that he wished to visit. Then as they came from the courtyard they saw a small, twisting, stone staircase leading upwards from one of the side corridors. It was very unlike the grand staircase which they had passed earlier, and swiftly, without speaking and on tiptoe so as to make as little noise as possible, they climbed up it.

They reached a passage which was lit by only one small electric light. It was obvious that this part of the villa was not intended to attract visitors.

"Up again," Bing whispered, and now they were on the second floor and again it was practically in darkness save at the very end where there were lights and, as Melina guessed, a link with the grander and more important parts of the villa.

Bing moved towards the lighted part of the corridor and opened the first door he came to. He switched on the light and Melina saw it was a bedroom, well furnished but not expensively so.

It was quiet, for the window obviously opened on to the back of the house and after a quick glance round Bing said:

"Stay here and wait for me. If anyone comes, say you felt faint and I have gone to try and get some aspirin for you."

"But, Bing . . ." Melina protested, only to see his back disappearing through the door so swiftly that it seemed almost as if he had wings on his heels.

The room seemed airless because the window was closed. Melina opened it feeling that if anyone did discover her they would think it strange that she had not tried to get some air into the room.

It was impossible to see much from the window but she thought that against the skyline she could discern a part of the hill from which they had surveyed the villa earlier in the day. Then she moved hastily away from the window in case anyone should come in and think it odd that she should be looking out.

She considered lying down on one of the beds and then changed her mind. There was something undignified about being found lying flat. Instead she sat down in an armchair, put a cushion comfortably behind her back and shut her eyes.

She might be looking relaxed, but she knew that every muscle and every nerve in her body was strained to listen for Bing's return. She felt curiously like tears with the sheer frustration of having to wait and do nothing while he went alone to face whatever danger there was. And then she began to think of the small boy and to pray for his safety.

"Let Bing find him! Oh, God! Please let Bing find him."

How long she prayed and waited she did not know. Suddenly she heard someone coming and was ready to jump for joy at the fact that Bing was returning. And then, just as she was about to move, something in the heaviness of the tread and the firmness and steadiness of the footsteps told her that it could not be Bing.

She closed her eyes and braced herself. The footsteps came nearer, paused for a moment and then passed on. She looked up and with a sense of dismay realised that the draught from the window must have opened the door wider than Bing had intended. He had left it nearly closed; now it stood wide open and anyone who had passed must have seen her.

It was not that it mattered particularly because she had been lying looking exhausted, as they had planned. At the same time if it was a servant why had he not asked her what was the matter or if he could help? Vaguely she felt something was wrong, but she did not know what to do about it.

She crossed the room and pushed the door back, leaving it just ajar as Bing had done. Then she went back to her chair to sit listening. She had not been there long before she heard footsteps returning. This time there were more of them; two people, perhaps three, were coming and there was still no sign of Bing.

The footsteps came nearer and nearer and now the door was burst open; someone stood there looking at her. Slowly with a tremendous effort to appear unhurried, she opened her eyes.

Moulay Ibrahim was looking down at her. She recognised him immediately, but she had not expected him to be so tall. He seemed to tower over her and she felt in her heart a sudden fear that was physical.

"Why are you here?" he asked in French.

She realised as he spoke that he must be perturbed otherwise the courtesy of the East would have prevented him from speaking so peremptorily. With what she hoped looked a natural movement Melina put her hands across her eyes.

"I'm so ... sorry," she said, "but I ... I felt ... faint. In fact I ... think I ... must have fainted ... for a moment. My ... my husband has gone to ... to get assistance."

"Why are you on this floor?"

The words were sharp and now Melina managed to force a smile to her lips as she sat upright and then got slowly to her feet.

"You are Moulay Ibrahim, aren't you?" she asked. "Thank you for ... a lovely party. I am ashamed at ... at behaving so stupidly."

"How did you get up here?" Moulay Ibrahim asked in a quieter, less aggressive tone.

"We were ... exploring your beautiful house," Melina said still with a smile on her lips. "It is so very lovely; you have such wonderful treasures. I wanted to ... to see every part of it."

"It is yours to command."

It was the facile, easy reply spoken not only in French but with the gallantry of a Frenchman. And now Moulay Ibrahim looked over his shoulder.

"Where is your husband?"

"I have no idea," Melina answered. "I asked him to

111

see if he could find someone who could provide me with an aspirin."

Moulay Ibrahim said something in Arabic to the two servants who were standing behind him. They looked frightened, Melina thought, and she guessed that one of them should have been on duty on the small spiral staircase up which she and Bing had come without opposition.

They sprang to obey his command and now, as Moulay Ibrahim turned back to her, she looked up into his face and thought it was one of the most handsome and yet most sinister faces she had ever seen.

There was something in his eyes that reminded her of a hooded snake and yet his features, thickened a little with middle-age, were still as perfect as those of a Greek statue and he might, when he was younger, have been sculptured as a dark-skinned Apollo. But there was an aura of evil around him. It was not visible, but Melina could feel it as surely as if she were clairvoyant.

"What is your name?"

His voice was low and she had the feeling that if he wished he could use it hypnotically.

"Melina Cutter."

"I seem to have seen you before!"

"But of course, we have been here all the evening," Melina answered.

"No, no, not this evening," he said with a frown between his eyes at the effort of memory. "Now I remember! You were looking out of a window in the town—the House of Rasmin."

She saw the suspicion leap into his eyes and tried to dispel it.

"I saw you on your black horse," she said. "I had no idea who you were, of course, but you looked like something out of the *Arabian Nights*."

"You were in the House of Rasmin." Moulay Ibrahim said slowly and almost reflectively, as if he talked to himself.

"Was that the name of the shop?" Melina asked innocently. "We had visited almost every one in the

112

whole city, but that man—whatever he was called—had the best slippers of the lot. I bought three pairs—one pair for myself and two for my friends when I get home."

"And where is home?" Moulay Ibrahim asked.

Melina just prevented herself from saying, "London", and substituted: "New York. We're not often there," she added confidingly. "My husband loves travelling."

"Indeed!"

As if the mention of her husband evoked Moulay Ibrahim's suspicions as to what Bing was doing, he suddenly turned towards the door.

"I will bring you some aspirin," he said. "Wait here."

He went out and shut the door firmly behind him. Melina heard him give an order to someone in the corridor, and although she could not understand what was said she had the unmistakable feeling that he had given instructions that she was not to leave the room.

Now Moulay Ibrahim was gone, she put her fingers up to her cheeks and found that her hands were trembling. There was something overwhelming and overpowering about his personality. There was also that impression of evil which told her that this man would baulk at nothing, not even murder, to get what he wanted.

Bing was in danger and she could do nothing to help him. If only she could warn him that Moulay Ibrahim was on his track. She moved across the room on tiptoe and put her ear against the door. Yes, she was certain she could hear someone breathing outside. Moulay Ibrahim was making sure that she did not escape while he searched the place for Bing.

Melina had to calculate how long Bing had been gone; ten minutes? A quarter of an hour? It was difficult to know; and now she could make no pretense of sitting and waiting but moved restlessly about the room. Where could he be? What could he be doing? Supposing Moulay Ibrahim caught him? What would happen? Would they kill him quickly and drop his body down a well? Or would they take him prisoner? Anyway, she was certain of one thing—that a prisoner of Moulay Ibrahim would never escape.

It seemed to her now that the whole project had been ridiculous and absurd. Why should Bing, an unarmed, solitary Englishman, think he could possibly rescue a child on whom so much rested that he was guarded day and night with the utmost vigilance. And if he was in the villa, what would Bing gain by the knowledge? He was not likely to be able to rescue him single-handed.

It was mad! Mad from the start to the finish! Melina felt exasperated and furious that she had not protested sooner at what she felt was just a bit of masculine obstinacy and conceit on Bing's part. Bring in the military; bring in the police, or anyone but don't try to achieve alone what was utterly and completely impossible.

She heard someone coming down the corridor and hastily re-seated herself in the chair. The handle of the door turned. Moulay Ibrahim came into the room.

"There is apparently no sign of your husband in the house," he said and his voice was sharp. "Can you describe to us what he looks like?"

"He is about medium height," Melina said slowly. "Brown hair; clean shaven. He has a very nice face! He was wearing a white dinner jacket."

"So are several hundreds of my other guests," Moulay Ibrahim said.

"Well, I suppose he looks rather American," Melina said.

"American?"

It was a question and Melina nodded her head.

"Yes, I am English, but my husband is American. We haven't been married very long. Where can he have got to, do you imagine?"

It seemed as if the fact that Bing was American had lightened the tension. Moulay Ibrahim's voice was certainly more affable and Melina pressed home her advantage.

114

"I expect he's got lost looking at your pictures or something," she said. "It would be just like Bing to forget all about me."

"Well, we must certainly see if we can find him for you." Moulay Ibrahim said.

"I suppose he wouldn't have gone back to the town to buy me some aspirin?" Melina suggested.

"It seems a long way to go for anything so simple," Moulay Ibrahim replied. "He had only to ask one of my servants. Several of them speak English and I'm sure they could have procured exactly what he wanted with very little difficulty."

"Perhaps he felt embarrassed to trespass on your hospitality," Melina said. "It would be just like him to go miles to get me something I wanted. He's so considerate and kind although he's a little absent-minded. I think Americans make the best husbands in the world."

She stopped speaking to look up into Moulay Ibrahim's face and she saw, partly in relief and partly with apprehension, that the suspicion had gone from his eyes and that a very different expression had taken its place.

There was something in the way he looked at her, something in the faint smile at the corners of his mouth, which told her that here was danger of another sort.

"You are very pretty," Moulay Ibrahim said softly. "Your husband is a lucky man."

His eyes flickered over her red hair and the soft curves of her figure so that she felt as if he mentally undressed her.

She turned quickly away from him to look out of the window into the darkness.

"I cannot think where my husband can be," she said.

"Tomorrow will you let me show you a little of the East as it should be seen?" Moulay Ibrahim asked.

She knew it was an invitation with a double meaning and that it insinuated far more than the simplicity of

115

the words. She tried to answer lightly, moving a little further away from him.

"I don't know if we shall be here tomorrow. We have stayed longer than we intended so that we could come to your party."

"If you are here, may I send a car to fetch you?"

"I shall have to ask my husband."

"Your husband is not included in the invitation!"

There was no disguising now the sudden light in his eyes nor the expression on his lips. Melina drew herself up.

"I don't think I understand you," she said.

"I think you do," he replied. "No woman can really be stupid when it concerns her own charms, and you are so very lovely."

"I am flattered that you should think so," Melina answered, her voice cold.

He put out his hand suddenly and took hers. Her fingers were very small and ineffective as they struggled against his.

"Do not fight me," he said. "I think it was *karma* that we should meet. I saw your face at the window and it was imprinted in my mind. The face of an angel or, rather, of a woman so lovely that the dark streets of Fez were for one moment transformed. I never thought to see you again and yet here you are in my house— and we are alone."

"I don't suppose we shall be alone for more than a moment or two," Melina said. "Even if my husband has gone into the town, he should be back by now."

"Perhaps he has lost his way," Moulay Ibrahim said. "Do not worry about him. Let this moment work its own magic. Cannot you feel how my heart is beating, how my whole being yearns for the smile from your lips? Look at me!"

Without consciously meaning to do so Melina looked up. He was trying to hypnotise her, she thought, seeing his dark eyes, large and strangely penetrating, looking down into hers compellingly, while his hand seemed to be drawing her closer and ever closer.

"Look at me," he was saying again in a low insisting tone, but with a superhuman effort she shook herself free, pulling her hand violently from his and running to the window to draw in deep breaths of the night air.

"Go away!" she cried. "Go away from me at once. I know what you are doing."

"Why are you afraid?"

Now his voice was caressing and he was coming nearer to her slowly and purposefully. She wanted to scream, but she felt as if her voice died in her throat. Moulay Ibrahim was standing just behind her and she felt that at any second his arms would be round her. With a lithe movement she evaded him.

"I can hear my husband," she said. "He is coming!" Running across the room she dragged open the door.

There were two men on either side of it, but she did not stop to look at them. Instead she ran with all the speed she could command down the corridor towards the brightly lighted landing at the far end. She only paused and looked back when she reached the top of the grand staircase and could see the crowds milling around the hall below and climbing the red carpet to the first floor.

Moulay Ibrahim was standing outside the door of the bedroom she had just left, speaking to his servants. He was making no attempt to follow her; he was not even looking in her direction and yet she had the uneasy feeling that he had by no means forgotten her.

Bing! Where could Bing be? If she left now, how could she ever find him again? She had a sudden idea and descending the stairs to the first floor, she ran along the corridor which was directly below the one she had just left, until she found the entrance to the twisting, stone staircase up which they had originally climbed.

She listened for a moment in case she should hear Moulay Ibrahim or one of his servants descending that way, and when there was no sound she slipped off her shoes and ran down the stairs in her stockinged feet until she reached the ground floor.

In a few seconds she found herself not in the court-

117

yard, as she had expected, but outside the back of the house. She put on her shoes and then stood for the moment confused. She had thought somehow that she would find Bing or signal to him from the courtyard, but this was a different part of the villa.

There were lights in some of the lower windows, but the top ones were in darkness. It was then, just as she was about to turn and go back, that she saw something silhouetted against the skyline. There was a man on the parapet of the roof; a man with his shoulders hunched moving swiftly towards the corner of the house. It might be one of Moulay Ibrahim's servants and yet she had a feeling that it was not.

She stood for a moment striving to see if it was Bing, and wondering how she could signal to him. And then a trick that her father had taught her many years ago, of whistling with two fingers in her mouth, came to her mind. It was an errand-boy's whistle, a whistle that one could expect to find only in the back streets of London.

She put her fingers between her lips and blew. Just for a moment the figure against the roof seemed to keep absolutely still and then a face looked over the parapet and something in the shape of the head told her unmistakably it was Bing.

He whistled back and pointed to where the parapet ended and she thought she understood what he meant. She started to walk quietly past the lighted windows. The ground was flagged with tiles, there was a sudden stench from a dustbin and she knew that some of the rooms she was passing must be the kitchens.

A cat started out of the shadows and startled her. Now she was nearing the corner of the house and she looked up searching for Bing against the skyline. There was no sign of him and she was ready to scream with fear until she saw him swarming down a drainpipe— coming down hand over hand with an agility which made her think of a sailor descending the mast of an old sailing ship.

She held her breath as she watched him. Supposing he slipped? Or supposing he landed beside her with a broken leg? Instead he jumped the last few feet to the ground and came hurrying to her side.

"Why did you leave the room?" he asked.

"I can't tell you that now," she said, "but we must get away."

"Is anything the matter?" he asked, surprised at the agitation in her voice.

"How can you ask that?" she questioned, her tone almost hysterical. "Did you . . . did you find the child?"

"We mustn't stay here talking," he said. "Let us go back to the lawns."

"No!" she answered. "No, we mustn't do that. Don't you understand? They are looking for you."

"Who is?"

She had never heard Bing speak in quite that manner.

"Moulay Ibrahim and his servants."

"Why didn't you say so?" he said. "Did he suspect who you were?"

"He was very suspicious at first," Melina said, "And then . . . then he had other . . . ideas which distracted him."

"What ideas?"

"He . . . he tried to hypnotise me. Oh, Bing! Let's get away."

"The devil he did!"

Bing was surprised. This was something, she thought, that he had not anticipated.

"All the same," he said after a moment, "I don't want to leave now."

"Why not?" Melina asked. "The child is there?"

"I know which room he is in," Bing said. "Later on in the evening there might be a chance."

"I doubt it," Melina said. "They are on their guard now. I told him that you might have gone to the town to get me some aspirin. It was the only excuse I could think of why you were away so long."

"That was clever of you."

There was warm approval in his voice.

119

"I don't want to see Moulay Ibrahim again," Melina said. "I am afraid of him. Bing, he is a horrible man."

"That is the understatement of the week," Bing agreed with a hint of laughter in his voice.

He was drawing her away from the house as they spoke down into a part of the garden which had not been lit. They could hear the sound of the music, they could see the lights in the distance, but they were apart from it all like spectators watching a scene set on a distant stage.

"Bing what are you going to do?" Melina asked.

"The boy is in the third room from the end on the top corridor," Bing answered. "The windows look out to the side and not either to the front or the back of the house. He has guards outside his door and there is, too, someone with him. I could hear the child talking."

"With so many people to guard him what can you do?" Melina asked.

"That is what I am trying to figure out," Bing answered. "It's not going to be easy."

"It's impossible!" Melina said. "Did anyone see you?"

"I'm not certain," Bing replied. "I had to pass one servant on my way and I told him in Arabic that he was wanted below. He obeyed me, but if he has reported what I said it might cause trouble."

"Then we have got to get away," Melina said. "Can't you see that nothing you can do now will be of the slightest help?"

She stopped. Bing was feeling in all his pockets.

"Damn!" he exclaimed suddenly. "Damn! I thought I heard something fall."

"What is it?" Melina asked.

"My glasses," he said. "The dark glasses I wear in the daytime. They were in my pocket. I never knew when I might not want to be disguised and when I was shinning up on that roof I had to go through a trapdoor in the ceiling—it was the only way I could get up. I caught my coat. I thought I heard something fall behind me."

"Where did you drop them?" she asked.

"Not far from the boy's room," he answered grimly and they both knew what this admission meant.

"They will know somebody's been there," Bing went on with a sigh in his voice, "and it won't take Moulay Ibrahim long to put two and two together and realise that it was a certain Mr. Cutter whose wife chose a second floor bedroom in which to feel faint."

As he spoke they both looked back at the house. A door at the back by the kitchens suddenly opened and the golden light came streaming out. Against it they saw two or three servants.

"They are looking for you," Melina said quickly. "I know it. I am absolutely certain of it. Come on, we've got to get away."

"How could I have been such a damned fool?" Bing asked bitterly.

"You couldn't help it," Melina soothed him. "It's the sort of thing that might have happened to anyone."

"It's the kind of stupidity which costs lives," Bing said grimly. "And I think you are right; they are looking for us. Come on! In amongst the guests is much the safest place."

He took her hand and they ran through the unlit part of the garden until, panting a little, they joined the guests wandering among the flowers. Now in the brilliance of the floodlit house and the lighted gardens they both instinctively looked up at the villa.

Moulay Ibrahim had come on to the terrace. They could see him standing talking to a rather more elaborately dressed servant who Melina had guessed was a kind of major-domo. He was giving instructions; his arm went out in a wide gesture embracing, it seemed to her, even the car park on the further side of the house.

"They are going to search everywhere," she said breathlessly. "We've got to get away."

Bing didn't pause to argue. He started to lead her at quite a swift pace through the perambulating guests.

"Bing, where are you going?"

121

It was Lileth Schuster who cried out to him and now she stepped forward to stand in front of them both.

"I forgot to ask you," she said, "where are you staying? There's such a crowd here we may easily lose each other and I must see you tomorrow."

"We're at the Jasmin Hotel," Bing answered.

"Oh, so are we," Lileth cried. "How wonderful! I'll telephone you tomorrow morning. We must make plans, lots of plans."

These, Melina thought, obviously would not include her because she looked and spoke only to Bing.

"Yes, telephone tomorrow morning," Bing said abruptly, and turned to pass on.

"You're not going surely?" Lileth asked. "I want to dance with you again—and I know Ambrose has only been waiting to find Melina."

"We will meet you both in a quarter-of-an-hour at the fountain," Bing said. "We've got someone we have to see at this moment."

Lileth turned away satisfied and Melina gave an hysterical little laugh as, free of her, they hurried on towards their car. They got into it and Bing started up the engine.

"Suppose they stop us at the gate?" Melina asked.

"They're not going to," Bing answered. "Hold tight!"

He drove the car towards the main gate. As they reached it a servant, who had obviously been talking on the telephone to the house, stepped out as if to stop them. Bing shot past him. The car almost took his arm off and the man stepped back just in time.

"Look back," Bing commanded. "What's he doing?"

"He is staring after us," Melina reported. "No, I think he's gone to the telephone."

"We've just done it," Bing said.

He started to drive quickly down the hill towards the town, then suddenly he went slower, stopped and began to back into a sandy side-track which led off the tar-mac road.

"What are you doing?" Melina asked apprehensively.

"I want to wait here a moment," Bing said. "Do you mind?"

"No, of course not," Melina said. "But why?"

"You'll see," Bing answered. "At least, I think so."

He switched off the engine and lights and they sat in silence. Melina wanted to ask questions, but something in Bing's attitude prevented her.

Then suddenly there was the sound of a car coming down the road and she saw him bend forward. It was travelling fast; a big limousine with its lights full on despite the moonlight which made everything very clear.

It flashed past them and Melina saw a chauffeur in the front and what appeared to her to be two men in the back. She heard Bing utter an exclamation beneath his breath and realised that this was what he had been waiting for.

"I thought there were two men in the back of that car," she hazarded, hoping he would appease her curiosity.

"Yes, there were two men," he answered. "Two men with a small boy sitting between them."

8

"What do we do now?" Melina asked in a whisper.

"We get the hell out of here!" Bing replied grimly.

He got out of the car, saying as he did so, "I'll have a look round and see if the coast's clear."

Melina suddenly felt terrified of being left alone. She scrambled out of her side of the car and tried to run after Bing who was already climbing up the rocky incline which rose sharply behind the car towards a number of stunted trees. As the ground was sandy Melina's satin shoes were soon full of grit and sand, and by the time she reached Bing's side she was limping.

He reached out his hand and caught hold of her arm above the elbow as she came up to him.

"Keep low," he said. "I want to see if there is a car parked at the end of the road."

Bending almost double and drawing Melina along with him, Bing began to move through the trees. They had gone only a short way when the sound of an engine behind them made him turn his head. Just for a moment he was still and then, as his fingers tightened on her arm until it was painful, Melina gave a little gasp of horror.

Coming down the road from the Villa was a high vehicle fitted with a strong search-light which swung from side to side, revealing a large area of the land on either side of the road. It was only a question of seconds, Melina thought, before the light would pick them up and reveal them standing defenceless on the raised ground.

Bing's white tuxedo and her pale-blue evening dress were silhouetted against the trees and the darkness of the sky; then, as something like terror crept over her, she was knocked off her feet.

She felt herself falling, felt the ground hard and painful beneath her shoulders as the weight of Bing's body sprawling on top of her left her breathless.

For a few seconds she was unable to think, unable to realise anything except the hurt of her shoulders and the difficulty she was having in breathing. For a moment, she decide later, her senses were almost blacked out.

Then she was aware of Bing's arms round her, of his body pressing hard and still harder against her breasts and her legs, and of a light, brilliant and searching, playing on the trees above them.

"They must see us, they must!" Melina thought desperately and knew with the sharpness of fear that this was indeed the danger Bing had warned her about. She held her breath as she strained her ears to listen, then tried to breathe again and heard a rasping sound come from between her lips.

"Quiet!" Bing murmured the word between his teeth. Melina heard him and was rigid again.

Now there were voices coming nearer to them; two men talking together in Arabic. They had found the car, she thought in a panic and with a kind of dull despair, for the men had only to look upwards to see them both.

She realised now that Bing had thrown her down into a kind of trench or ditch made, perhaps during the rainy season, but at the moment filled only with sand and stones. It was not deep and she was terrified lest Bing's white tuxedo should be visible.

The voices beneath them were loud and clear. It was obvious that the men were standing by the car, and though Melina could not understand what they said, she could guess by the intonation of their voices that they were discussing the ownership of the empty car and were suspicious of its presence there.

She was aware of Bing's heart beating against her breast and she knew by the manner in which he strove to press her lower and yet lower into the ground, that he too was afraid.

She began to think that her whole body would break beneath him. The pain of his weight and the stones piercing her shoulders and back were almost unbearable, until she heard the voices beneath them receding, and knew that the men were walking back to their own vehicle. She heard the engine start up and then, suddenly, the light which had enveloped the trees and terrain above them was gone and there was a darkness which brought a relief too great for words.

Melina felt Bing draw a deep breath which seemed to come from the uttermost depths of his being, and for the first time she looked up at him, his face directly above hers, their eyes only a few inches apart. The search-light no longer illuminated everything, but in the light of the moon she could see the dark outline of his head and his eyes shining as they looked down into hers.

"Good girl."

His words were very low. She felt herself glow at the praise in his tone, and then suddenly and so unexpectedly that her whole body was tense with surprise, his mouth was on hers.

He kissed her harshly. His lips were hard and seemed to have no warmth in them, but hers were soft and unresisting because she was breathless and utterly unprepared.

It seemed to Melina that his kiss was almost a blow, given without desire and yet with a passion that was somehow part of the danger through which they had just passed.

"Bing!"

She was able to breathe the word as his lips were lifted from hers; and then, before she could say more, he was on his feet dragging her up after him. She wanted to stop and think, but this was obviously not Bing's intention. He pulled her, her feet slipping and slithering in the sand, behind a clump of trees. Hiding there, he whispered:

126

"I won't be a few minutes."

"What are you going to do? Oh, Bing, don't leave me!" Melinda pleaded. But she found herself speaking to the air, for he had already gone.

She crouched down behind the tree trunks, feeling there were eyes everywhere. At any moment, she told herself, the vehicle with the search-light might return and then she would be mesmerised like a rabbit in the headlights and, unable to escape from them, be mown down.

Now there was only silence, except that far away in the distance she fancied that she could hear faint sounds of music. It seemed as if, on leaving the Villa, she had cut herself off from civilisation and now she was at the mercy of the savagery of the jungle.

She put her hand to the back of her left arm and found it was bleeding. A stone would have done that, she thought, and imagined that her back was in the same state. Her whole body ached. She was conscious, too, that her mouth felt as if it also was bruised.

She raised her hand as if to touch her lips and, as she did so, was acutely conscious of the silence and her own isolation.

Bing? Where had he gone? Why had he left her alone? By what seemed an almost superhuman effort she prevented herself from springing to her feet and calling out his name. Why was he so long?

She had a sudden vision of herself being left alone because Bing thought he could travel more quickly or obtain his objective better without her. She imagined herself waiting for him until the dawn came and she was discovered by Moulay Ibrahim's men and taken back to the Villa to be interrogated by him.

She remembered the Sheik's face, the cruel lines of his mouth, the hardness of his eyes. She shut her eyes and could imagine all too clearly by what methods he would obtain any information he required.

"No, no, don't leave me!" She whispered the words into the night and opened her eyes to find Bing was already at her side.

127

"Why have you been so long? What have you been doing?"

In her relief at his appearance, she was angry rather than glad to see him.

In answer, he threw a bundle down at her feet.

"Get into this, and quickly."

"What is it?"

She looked at the shapeless white bundle on the ground and realised that he had another in his hands.

"It is a djellabah," he answered, "You'll find a yashmak there and also a pair of baboush."

Melina unrolled the bundle and saw a black yashmak and a pair of worn native slippers and raised her face to Bing. She thought that he was watching her, but, instead, he had already taken off his white tuxedo and was pulling at his collar and tie.

Obediently, because she did not want to hinder him, Melina picked up the djellabah and began to put it on. Fortunately her father had possessed a yashmak and various other articles of women's clothing amongst the souvenirs he had brought back from many places in the East and she had often amused herself when she was a child, by dressing up and being told by him exactly how such things should be worn.

She had always found herself defeated by the Indian sari, the folds of which never looked as graceful on her as they did on those who were born to wear them. But the shapeless Moroccan costume, which made all women look like bundles of washing with a towel over their heads, had been the easiest disguise of all.

Melina slipped the gauze veil below her eyes and found also in the folds of the djellabah a metal circle which held the headdress in place. This only left the baboush, and as Melina picked them up she heard Bing's voice sharp and authoritative, saying:

"Get your stockings off and give them to me with your shoes."

Melina lifted the djellabah, undid her suspenders and pulled off her nylons. She had a moment's regret as she held them out to Bing, remembering they were her best

128

pair; and then, with something like a grimace, she thought how ridiculous it was to think of anything so trivial at a moment like this.

Bing was digging a hole in the sand with his hands and when it was deep enough he pressed the white tuxedo down into it. He covered it up and dug another hole, into which he put Melina's evening shoes and stockings.

He stood up and she saw that he was already dressed in native costume, a long black burnous covered a robe of grey striped cotton. There was a turban wound round his head, and in some curious way his face had assumed the calm inscrutability of an Arab.

"Come!"

Bing held out his hand and drew Melina from the trees. She followed him, feeling strange and uncomfortable in her enveloping robe. She was conscious a moment or so later that the yashmak was cutting into her nose, making her feel hot despite the fact that a few moments earlier she had been cold with fear. The baboush slapped against her feet and she was in danger of losing them, until she remembered the shuffling walk of the native women and tried to copy it.

They moved along the top of the bank to where the trees were before Melina asked:

"Are you going towards the Villa? Isn't that dangerous?"

"On the contrary," Bing replied. "You can see there is a crowd hanging round the gates to watch the guests arrive and depart. Two other curious natives will not be noticed. Keep your head bowed modestly and your hands hidden. Remember you always walk a few paces behind me as befits an obedient and submissive wife."

"What about the car?" Melina asked.

"Forget it!" Bing said briefly. "We have no further use for it."

There was something in his voice which seemed to give her a little pang of pain or perhaps apprehension. He was so unconcerned about something costly for which he now had no need. Would he be like that

129

about anyone he knew—a friend, or even someone he loved?

As she asked herself the question, Melina knew that the answer was of vital importance to her personally. Bing had loved Lileth Schuster. Would he be ruthless where she was concerned now that she wanted and needed him? Would he be equally ruthless to any other woman?

They were moving slowly towards the Villa, in a few moments they would reach the main road and could walk more easily towards the lighted gates.

It seemed to Melina as if this private question within herself superseded all the danger and even the terror and fear of Moulay Ibrahim and those like him. Bing might be fighting them, but, for her, he had become not someone dedicated to a mission, not a fighter pitting his strength against frightening and unknown odds, but a man who had kissed her.

Under the cheap gauze which hid her mouth she could feel her lips throbbing and burning because they had known the touch of Bing's mouth. Why had he done it? He was not in love with her, she knew that. Up to now he had not even seemed to be attracted to her, and yet, hard and harsh though his kiss had been, it had awakened a flame within herself which she could no longer deny.

Did she love him? Had she loved him long before this happened? Had her very fear of him been part of her love? She could find no reply to these questions. She only knew with a kind of madness that her lips wanted to touch his again, that she wanted to feel his heart beating against her breast.

They reached the road. It was a relief from the sand and frequent stones to feel the smooth hard surface of it, but it was a very temporary relief. Bing crossed the road and, taking once again to the rough terrain, turned away from the Villa and started the downward descent of the hill which led towards Fez.

"Do you think anyone noticed us?" Melina breathed.

"If they did, we shall know in a few seconds," he replied.

But there were no shouts or cries after them nor the sound of a motor-bicycle coming from the Villa where Melina could see, quite clearly now, a great crowd of natives gathered as spectators.

"The party is over as far as we are concerned," Bing said, with a touch of laughter in his voice.

Melina wondered how he could be so gay, but it was difficult to question him as she was intent on keeping her baboush on her feet and, at the same time, trying not to fall headlong over the boulders and cactus plants which were hard to see, even in the moonlight.

After what seemed to her hours of pain and exhaustion, they finally reached the outside of the great high, age-old wall which encircled the native town. Once in the shadows Melina stopped and lifted up one of her feet to rub it ruefully.

"My back was bleeding after lying in the ditch," she said. "Now both my feet are in a disgusting state. Give me a moment to get my breath."

"I am sorry if I have rushed you," Bing replied.

"Your legs are longer than mine," Melina explained. "And I've walked into at least a dozen cacti. Where are we going, now?"

"To find the child," he answered, and she knew by the way in which he said it that his thoughts had been of no one else.

"How do you know where he has gone?"

"Someone will tell us," he replied. "Are you better now? We don't want to hang about here."

She heard the impatience in his tone and knew he resented her weakness. Because she wanted approval from him more than she had ever wanted it before from any man, she replaced her aching, blood-stained feet in the slippers and said meekly:

"I am ready."

They walked a long way round the wall until they came to a gate ornamented with the flags of the Arab Republic which led directly into the Medina. It was not

131

the gate Melina knew which was nearest to Rasmin's shop and her heart sank at the thought of the long walk down the twisted, cobbled alleys. But, after traversing only a few of the dark lanes with their shops shuttered for the night, Bing stopped in a doorway and rapped with his knuckles on the door.

Looking up, the high, windowless grimy house appeared to be in darkness. Melina longed to ask where they were and on whom they were calling, but she was wise enough not to speak, for behind the closed doors of the inscrutable tall houses who knew who might not be listening?

In the door a tiny grille covered with iron bars was opened; there was a glint of light and then they could see the eyes of a man looking at them inquiringly.

"By the Hand of Fatima," Bing whispered.

The grille was shut and the door opened just enough to allow them to pass through, then it was hastily closed behind them and Melina heard the sound of a bolt being driven home.

They were in a narrow passage, but she could see nothing until a curtain was pulled aside at the far end and she found herself following Bing into a small room which was furnished only with the low leather cushions of the East and an oil reading-lamp beside one of them on which rested a book.

Melina turned to look at the man who had let them in. He was young. He wore glasses and she had the quick impression that he was a student who was annoyed by their arrival which had interrupted his studies.

"Your Father told me to come to you if it was absolutely necessary," Bing said in French.

"He told me to expect you," the younger man replied. "As a matter of fact he is here himself. He had a premonition that you would need him."

"He is right," Bing answered. "We need him badly."

"I will fetch him."

The young man went from the room and Bing turned to Melina.

132

"Things are going well," he said. "Almost too well. I am a little afraid of our good fortune."

"But I cannot see anything good about it," Melina said. "What are we going to do now without a car, without any luggage?"

"It will all be seen to," Bing said lightly.

She felt almost irritated that he could speak with such inconsequence; but there was no time to say anything more because the tall youth returned to the room. Behind him came Rasmin.

"Hamdullilah," Rasmin ejaculated, which Melina knew meant, "Thanks to the Lord".

"We have got to work quickly," Bing answered. "I saw the child, but was unable to do anything and now they have taken him away. Where will they have gone?"

"One of my friends reported what had happened half an hour ago. You have been a long time getting here," Rasmin said.

"I had to move slowly," Bing replied with a little smile in the direction of Melina.

Thinking of her torn and bleeding feet and of the manner in which they had almost raced down the side of the hill towards the city, Melina could have hit him; but, before she could say anything, Bing asked quickly:

"Where have they gone?"

"To Marrakesh," Rasmin replied.

"You are certain of this?"

"The chauffeur who drove the car was told to have enough petrol in his tank for such a journey."

"That is good enough," Bing approved. "But how do we get there?"

"The roads are being watched," Rasmin answered.

"I am sure of it," Bing replied. "A vehicle with a search-light on the top nearly discovered us. It is stationed at the cross roads."

"So everyone who leaves the Villa must pass it," Rasmin muttered. "As we all know, there is no other road."

133

"Do you think they will suspect us of having come here on foot?" Bing asked.

"Not here," Rasmin replied, "but there is a beggar outside my door who has been there all day. That is why I visited my son by a route known only to myself, over the rooftops."

"And as we cannot get to Marrakesh over the roofs, how then?" Bing enquired.

"By bus," Rasmin replied.

"Rasmin, you are a genius!" Bing exclaimed. "But our disguise has got to be good."

Melina found the eyes of all three men on her. After a long scrutiny Bing said slowly:

"Many Riffians have, like the Irish, red hair, blue eyes, snub noses and freckles. Give her kohl round the eyes, henna her nails and the palms of her hands and she'll pass without much difficulty—but my outfit had better be perfect."

"Abdullah will see to that," Rasmin answered.

He produced a small bottle of kohl from a cupboard and, drawing Melina's yashmak gently from her face, started work on her eyes. A small boy, little more than a child, brought mint tea and there were small almond biscuits which Rasmin encouraged Melina to eat, saying it might be long before she had further food.

He darkened the skin of her hands and arms, telling her that while the Riffians might have fair skin on their faces, their hands were used to work and were therefore exposed to the sun.

The bronze henna looked strange on Melina's nails after the pink lacquer she ordinarily used had been removed, and Rasmin coloured the palms of her hands and the soles of her feet, exclaiming as he did so at the bruises and cuts she had incurred in her encounter with the cacti and from trying to keep up with Bing.

It all seemed to take a long time, but, actually only half an hour had passed before Bing returned with his skin darkened and wearing different native clothes which, Rasmin explained, proclaimed him as coming from a part of the country which few of the passengers on the bus would have visited.

Bing gulped down a cup of mint tea, and turning to Rasmin, held out his hand.

"Thanks to you, we may succeed, my old friend," he said.

"Inshallah!" Rasmin replied, which Melina had learnt meant, "if God will it this way, let it be so".

She was too shy to attempt to speak in Arabic, so she said "Thank you" in French to Rasmin, to his son and to the small boy who had brought them in tea who, she gathered, was a grandson.

Then in the darkness they slipped silently out of the door and Abdullah led them through twisting, deserted lanes right across the city to where the buses were waiting outside the railway station.

"What time does it go?" Melina asked Bing in such a low voice that no one could have overheard her.

"Five o'clock," he answered.

"So early?"

"It is a long way to travel," Bing replied. "The buses, which are almost the only way in which the natives get about the country, stop at every village and hamlet and often because the driver wants a nap. Be prepared for your liver to be shaken up," he added as an afterthought.

Within sight of the station Abdullah faded away into the shadows in which they had come. Feeling naked and exposed, Bing and Melina walked across the open square where men were already setting out fruit stalls, and women carried from the well huge stone pots of water on their heads.

The bus for Marrakesh was waiting, besides several others which Melina guessed were not to go so far or leave so early. Already theirs was half full. Bing demanded two tickets in a voice that was part aggressive and part nervous as though he was afraid of so modern and swift a method of travel.

They got in. Bing going first with a masculine arrogance, spreading himself comfortably in the seat nearest

135

the window while Melina perched beside him next the aisle, her head downcast, her feet tucked beneath her seat.

A woman carrying a basket of eggs, another with two live chickens suspended by their legs, a commercial traveller with a number of worn suitcases, a family of two or three children and a Catholic priest, all entered one after another.

Outside, as daylight grew and the sun flooded over the city, people began to crowd the square. An open lorry packed with workers for a factory moved off amid shouts and catcalls.

Bing was sitting back comfortably at his ease, but Melina knew that underneath his air of bravado he was as afraid as she was that they might be stopped at this eleventh hour.

With a last word to a friend, wiping his mouth after the breakfast he had consumed, and spitting as he climbed into the front seat, the driver took his place. He glanced round at the passengers. Someone slammed-to the door at the back.

The engine started up, there was a back-fire and one of the veiled women at the back of the bus gave a scream of fright. A man laughed. The driver grated the gear into place and they were off.

"We've done it!" Melina wanted to cry the words out loud. Instead she kept still, with her head a little down, not daring to look at Bing.

It was then she felt his hand touch her, reassuringly, the approving touch of a man who wants to convey his gladness. Things had gone right!

She felt his hand for one moment and then he was looking out of the window apparently indifferent to her, absorbed only in the new sensation of travelling by bus, but in that fleeting moment Melina had known the answer to the question she had been asking herself all night.

She loved him. She loved Bing. Whatever he was, however much he had frightened her. She loved him and she could not deny her leaping heart.

136

9

Melina's head dropped forward on her chest and she awoke with a start. For a moment she could not think where she was; then the rattle of the bus over the rough roads, the stifling atmosphere all around her, the glass windows fogged with heat and smoke, brought everything flooding back to her mind.

It had been the longest day she could ever remember. They had moved at quite a good speed between stops, but every hour or so the passengers had disembarked to sit drinking mint tea in some fly-blown café, or to eat Arab food which Melina found extremely unappetising. There was no question of Bing and herself ordering anything else. So, because she was tired and hungry she forced herself to swallow mouthfuls of camel meat and other more anonymous dishes which smelt so disgusting that she dared not even guess their origin.

Bing had not spoken to her since they left Fez except to give a brief command to dismount from the bus or to mount it again, and she understood from watching the other couples that this was the usual behaviour of a Moslem to his wife.

Meekly she walked behind him when they disembarked, seated herself in the worst places in the cafés, which, fortunately, meant that she usually had her back to the other people in the room.

It was correct for her to keep her head bowed and to raise her yashmak only a fraction above her mouth when she ate; and she knew that the other Moslem men would, traditionally, not look in her direction for fear of insulting the man to whom she belonged. She felt that her anonymity was, therefore, easy to preserve and it gave her a sense of security.

Now, however, she realised with something of a shock that they were arriving in Marrakesh. Through the clear windscreen at the front of the bus she had a vision of high ramparts, red-gold in colour extending with geometrical perfection into the distance, and of a sky glorious in crimson, flame and yellow as the sun set behind the tall palm trees.

This was Marrakesh, she thought. The town which Winston Churchill loved. A city of a thousand date palms, enchanted parks and gardens of pomegranates and apricots.

She remembered now that the red ramparts were almost a thousand years old and, as they passed through them, she saw ahead Islam's most famous minaret, the Kutcubria, changing its colour even as she looked at it, from ivory to brown, from the pink of a seashell to the flaming red of the last rays of the setting sun.

She longed to speak to Bing, to ask questions. But she knew she could say nothing, only watch with fascination as the bus drew up in a great square filled with crowds of people.

There were shouts and exclamations from the other travellers as they waved to their friends or called out their excitement and appreciation of having arrived safely after what was to them a most dangerous journey; and then they were hurrying and crowding out of the bus and Melina and Bing, moving more slowly, were the last to descend.

The noise and confusion outside was almost overpowering. It was very hot. Melina could feel the sweat gathering on her forehead. As they moved through the crowd she found it difficult not to be pushed away from Bing by those too intent on peering at the amusements around them to look where they were going.

She had heard often enough of Djemma El Fna, the famous market-square in Marrakesh, and now that she saw it for herself it seemed even more incredible than the descriptions she had read so avidly in her father's books.

There were snake-charmers and fire eaters, acrobats from the Sous; daring Shleh boys with provocatively wiggling hips; grave-eyed medicine men advising customers on how to prolong their virility; sword dancers and Berber dancers; water-carriers with straw hats decorated with brightly coloured wool, and hundreds of beggars in patched tatters holding out supplicating hands to the tourists or to anyone else who would listen to them.

Melina was wide-eyed with interest and astonishment, but Bing moved purposefully through the crowd, seldom looking to right or left. This was the great El Dorado of the South, the destination to which camel caravans from the desert journeyed as they had done for a thousand years; but he was concerned with only one thing, his concentration pin-pointed on what he had come to find.

Melina kept up with him breathlessly. Now they were moving on the fringe of the crowd. Crossing the road, they came under the shadow of some great trees which overhung a crumbling wall. The swift twilight of the east had almost gone, darkness was falling. The minaret was already silhouetted against the sable sky in which the stars were coming out one by one.

There was a gap in the wall where the bricks had fallen away from the pavement into the garden beyond. Bing glanced quickly over his shoulder and climbed through it, leaving Melina to scramble after him.

In the privacy of the garden which lay beyond, he turned to give her his hand and to help her over the fallen stones until her feet touched softer ground. They had to force their way through some overgrown shrubs, the flowers of which gave off a sickly, almost overwhelmingly sweet fragrance. After a few moments they came to a tumbledown edifice with a pillared front.

The stars were brighter and the moon was rising. They were able to see quite clearly what lay round them.

"Where are we?" Melina asked in a whisper.

"Safe, I hope, for the moment," Bing answered.

There were two steps leading up to what appeared to be a small temple. Bing sat down on the top one, leant his back against the pillar and gave a sigh of exhaustion and relief before he stretched his arms above his head.

"I'm stiff," he said, "So must you be."

"Every bone in my body is aching," Melina answered. "But I am too thankful to be here to worry about it. What is this place?"

"A tomb," Bing told her. Melina gave a little start and he smiled.

"Relax," he said. "The occupant has been dead for hundreds of years and only the faithful believe that he walks these grounds at night. Anyway, his ghost, real or otherwise, will protect us now that it is dark from inquisitive strangers."

"Do you mean we are going to stay here?" Melina asked incredulously. She sat down beside Bing as she spoke and pulled off her yashmak. Her face was hot and wet and it was with a feeling of real pleasure that she was able to pull out her vanity case from beneath the enveloping folds of her robe and powder her nose.

"You don't mean to say that you've brought that with you?" Bing asked in an amused voice.

"Do you really think any woman would travel without her handbag?" Melina inquired. "I attached it to the belt of my dress."

Bing laughed and somehow the sound was human and comforting.

Melina put her vanity case away and turned towards him.

"I want to know what's going to happen," she said. "It has been ghastly being silent all day, longing to ask you questions but not daring to open my lips."

"A good lesson in femininity," Bing chuckled.

"Don't you dare say that!" Melina retorted. "After all those beastly meals and the discomfort of the bus, you at least owe me an explanation of what you intend to do now."

Bing looked across into the dark shadow of the trees.

"There is only one thing that concerns me," he said, and his voice was suddenly grave and deep.

"I know that," Melina said. "But how are we going to find him?"

"Someone will come for us here later on tonight, I hope," Bing said. "If they are not too afraid."

"And if they are?" Melina inquired.

"Then we shall have to work without them."

"If only we could make a plan," she cried, then stopped and looked at him, her eyes searching through the darkness to discern the expression on his face.

"You have a plan," she said accusingly.

". . . No," Bing answered, but he hesitated before he spoke and she did not believe him.

"Don't shut me out," Melina begged. "I'm in this with you. I have a right to know what you intend to do."

She thought with a kind of desperation that it would always be like this between them. Bing, reserved, taciturn, keeping his thoughts and feelings from her as if a wall as high as the red ramparts existed between them. "He doesn't trust women," she thought, and felt a sudden pang of loneliness and, at the same time, a desperate urge to prove her own worthiness to be trusted.

"Tell me, please tell me," she begged, only to know that her pleading was a mistake and that it had driven Bing further away from her for ever.

"There is nothing to tell," he answered. "You realise how difficult and discreet communications must be. Rasmin will have done what he can. It remains to be seen what support I will be given here."

"What about the hotel in Fez?" Melina asked. "What will they think when we do not return and they find all our clothes in the rooms we occupied and the bill left unpaid?"

"Do not worry about them," Bing answered. "Mr. and Mrs. Cutter were called to America at a moment's notice owing to the death of Mr. Cutter's father. Their

141

luggage was packed and sent to the airport to follow them on the next available aeroplane."

"And the car?" Melina asked. "Moulay Ibrahim's men will have reported that we left it there."

"It will have told them little," Bing replied. "The number plates will have been changed and a young man respected in the town will have been relating to his friends all day how he had to walk home having run out of petrol."

"You think of everything," Melina said as she had said it before, only to be quickly shushed into silence by Bing's raised hand.

"No compliments," he said quickly. "It's unlucky."

"What about our passports?" Melina asked.

"They are in my jacket pocket," Bing replied. "The ink has already faded and, on paper, you are no longer married to me."

Melina longed to reply that it was the one thing she wanted above all else. Then, like a nightmare from the past, there flashed before her eyes the petulant face of Lileth Schuster.

She could hear again the passion in her voice when she told Bing that she loved him. "Forget her," Melina longed to say to him. "Forget her for she is hard and cruel and will bring you only unhappiness."

She felt in that moment as if Bing was her son instead of a full-grown man; everything that was maternal in her longed to protect him, to save him from being hurt, to prevent his faith and love from being destroyed. She knew instinctively with each one of her five senses that Lileth Schuster was a bad woman, just as she knew that her own love was something real, true and enduring.

It wouldn't matter to her, she thought, if she had to live like this for the rest of her life—a despised woman in the Moslem creed, a creature of no importance and of no consequence—so long as she could be with Bing. Better this than the emancipation of the West if only, in fact, Bing could be with her and she love him, even if he never knew it.

Bing moved restlessly, Melina guessed that under his outward appearance of calm, he was anxious, tense and irritated by the inevitable delay of any action.

"Are you hungry?" he asked.

"Not for any Arab food," Melina replied, thinking with a sudden nausea of the sweet softness of the camel meat.

"Shall I see if I can get you some fruit?" Bing suggested, but she knew his solicitation was not really on her behalf but because he wanted to do something rather than sit waiting.

"Must you leave me here?" she asked. "Let me come with you."

"It would be safer for you to remain where you are," he said. "If you hear a noise, move into the tomb. No one will go there unless it is one of our friends."

"It does not look as if they treat a cemetery with much respect," Melina protested, thinking of the broken wall, the overgrown, unkept garden and the stained and cracked pillars against which they were leaning.

"*Qui sera sera,*" Bing remarked. "In Moslem countries everything is left in the hands of Allah. You must realise that by this time."

"I only wish I knew whether Allah was for us or against us in this project," Melina said a little sarcastically.

To her astonishment Bing answered her with complete seriousness.

"He is with us," he answered. "I have never doubted it for one moment since I undertook to find the boy."

For an instant they stared at each other. She thought in the moonlight that his expression was hard and then his hand came out and touched her cheek.

"You are a brave girl, Melina," he said. "Your father would have been proud of you."

She felt the sudden tears prick her eyes, both at the kindness of his voice and because he had praised her with words she valued above all others; then, before she could answer him, he had gone. The darkness swallowed him up. She was alone.

143

Because she was afraid, she retreated into the entrance of the tomb. There the air was stale and unpleasant and, after a moment she moved back again to the step, hoping that a little breeze would reach her to relieve the sultry heat which was still almost overpowering.

Melina longed to throw off her djellabah but knew it would be unwise. She wondered in what state her evening dress would be after this and thought with a little twist of her lips that if it could survive the heat and discomfort of the bus ride, it was the best advertisement that nylon could ever have.

It was then she realised how desperately tired she was, after more than twenty-four hours without sleep save for the cat-naps she had taken with a nodding head on the journey. She tried sitting with her back against the pillars and her legs outstretched in front of her, but it was too uncomfortable. Finally, she curled herself up on the top step of the temple and laid her aching head on her folded arms.

"I never thought I would want to sleep on the ground," was her last thought before she slept.

She was deep in a dreamless slumber in which every muscle and nerve in her body were utterly and completely relaxed when she felt herself being lifted into someone's arms. She was not afraid and some instinct stronger than thought told her it was Bing.

Without opening her eyes and still far away from consciousness, she felt him carrying her somewhere, his feet walking surely over the ground, his arms strong and protective and infinitely comforting.

She must have drifted away into oblivion because when he set her down very gently she had forgotten that he was carrying her. She was on something softer, something which gave beneath her body and yet was not a bed.

She had a sudden feeling as his arms drew away from her that he was going to leave her, and she wanted to cry out to him, to beg him to stay with her, to leave his arms around her and never let her go. But she was too tired, too far away to make the effort and only the thought was there amongst the clouds of slumber.

Then, as she felt herself alone and without him, she suddenly felt a pressure on her lips. It was gentle, sweet and undemanding, but like a streak of lightning the leaping flame which she had known before burnt within her and she knew a sudden ecstasy which made her feel as though the stars had dropped from the sky and settled in her eyes.

Her lips longed to hold on to his with passion and an insistence he could not refuse, but she was too far away. She struggled against the sleep which possessed her and as she did so the moment passed and his lips had gone.

She wanted to cry out for what she had lost, for the emptiness which was all that was left her, but she realised that he was settling himself beside her, his shoulder against her arm. His hip touched her hip and then his arm was thrown protectively across her. She could feel it there, heavy and yet giving her a sense of security such as nothing else could have done.

Instinctively she turned towards him. She laid her cheek against his shoulder and without conscious thought of what she was doing, cuddled her body against his. He drew her a little closer, and then he too slept. . . .

It must have been a cock that awakened her, a cock crowing triumphantly with all the strength and power of its tiny lungs. Melina opened her eyes and saw above her not a ceiling but the branches of trees bright with blossom, amongst which birds moved and fluttered and sang their morning song of delight.

She turned her head and saw that Bing lying close beside her was still sleep. For the first time she realised how young he was and now that he was off his guard she saw that he was also both sensitive and vulnerable. There was something very gentle in the curve of his lips. There was something boylike in this hollow of his cheek, in the sharp curve of his jaw.

His arm was still flung across her. Melina realised

145

that to move would awaken him, so she lay still, looking at him, wondering why out of all the men in the world she had had to give her heart to someone who loved another woman and for whom she herself only existed as a useful tool.

As if the scrutiny of her eyes roused him, Bing was suddenly alert. He awoke as men always do who live in the shadow of danger. His eyes opened and every nerve in his body awoke at the same time.

"Melina!" he exclaimed. "We should have been awake before this."

"What time is it?" she asked.

Bing glanced at the sun with its rays already percolating through the branches of the trees to turn the sandy ground beneath them into a carpet of gold.

"About six o'clock, I should think," he replied and rose to his feet.

Melina saw that they had been lying on a heap of grass such as the natives cut for their animals and which is carried in great high bundles on the backs of incredibly small donkeys. She too rose and noticed a little distance away at the end of the garden the tomb from which Bing must have carried her the night before.

It was then that she looked beyond the garden walls; she saw a sight which made her eyes widen, an exclamation of astonishment fall from her lips. The Atlas mountains, snow-capped and indescribably beautiful against the pale sky, were there in all their majesty.

"They are the most breathtaking mountains in the world," Bing said, following the direction of her eyes.

The contrast between the vivid, gleaming snow-capped peaks and the scarlet and purple bougainvillaea which ran riot over the walls of the garden was too glorious for description.

"I have seen them," Melina said softly. "At last I have seen them."

As if he had no time to be ecstatic over the beauties of nature, Bing put his hand on her shoulder and gave her a little push.

"You will find a broken fountain a little to the right of you," he said. "Do not drink the water but you can wash in it and then we will go in search of breakfast and our friends who have failed to come to our assistance."

Melina obediently turned in the direction in which he had pointed.

"Do not forget to put back your yashmak," he called after her as she left him.

She was not away a long time. Only long enough to wash her hands and face and ease her bruised feet in the stone bowl of the fountain into which a trickle of water still poured ceaselessly from a broken dolphin.

She would have liked to undress and bathe completely, but she knew that such an act was unthinkable and was only too grateful that at least her hands and feet were, for the moment, clean and free of the dust which had caked them, making the skin even darker than Rasmin had stained it.

She was very thirsty but she obeyed Bing's instructions not to drink the water, not even daring to wet her lips in case typhoid or some other dread disease should be waiting to attack her.

It was then that she remembered who had kissed her lips last night as she lay drugged with sleep and exhaustion, and a thrill ran through her at the thought that, once again, she had known the touch of his mouth. On neither occasion had it been the kiss of a lover, but it was enough for her aching heart that Bing had given her his lips.

Melina had a sudden urgent desire to hurry back to him, but when she reached the pile of grass on which they had slept, she saw that Bing was not alone. She stopped still, frightened and disconcerted.

The man was young; he wore a robe of striped grey cotton. There was a red fez stuck jauntily on his head and on his arm was the official brown armband of a government-appointed guide. The youth, for he was little more, and Bing were in deep conversation.

Melina stood irresolute until, as if he sensed her

147

presence Bing turned and saw her and beckoned her. She hurried towards them and saw the Arab's eyes appraising her closely, which told her that he knew she was not a Moslem but a European and therefore could be stared at.

"This is Ahmed," Bing said by way of introduction. "He could not come to us last night because his Father felt it would be unlucky to enter the sacred garden."

Ahmed smiled, showing a flash of gleaming white teeth.

"My Father is old and full of superstition," he said in good English. "I know, because I am young and better educated, that such things are nonsense. The dead do not rise from their tombs and there are no ghosts, but my Father still holds the money-bags and so I must obey him."

"It is enough that you have come today," Bing said courteously. "Do you bring me news?"

Ahmed shook his head.

"We have no idea where he whom you seek can be found. Those who serve Moulay Ibrahim are well paid and also afraid. They do not talk."

"Someone must know," Bing said. "Do not tell me that the East has lost the cunning of the serpent or that things can happen of which the market-place will not be chattering within a few hours."

Ahmed glanced over his shoulder.

"There are persons of whom it is unwise to ask questions," he said.

"Surely someone has seen the car arrive," Bing insisted. "Even if they did not see the boy, there were two men in the car which was a big expensive Mercedes, glittering with the badges of many countries. How could they pass unnoticed?"

Ahmed shrugged his shoulders.

"Undoubtedly it would have been seen, sir, but who would be brave enough to ask questions of those who would carry tales of their curiosity?"

It was obvious, Melina thought, that the youth was afraid. However willing he might be to help Bing, he had a sense of preservation which was not going to allow him to put his head in a noose by asking pertinent questions.

Bing obviously realised the same thing because there was a long pause before he spoke again, then he said:

"Moulay Ibrahim himself has not arrived?"

"No, of that I am certain," Ahmed answered. "It is easy to speak of him. He is a personality. Someone of great importance. He is generous too, to the dancers and beggars. They would have told if he had arrived."

"We can but wait and hope that when he does come," Bing said reflectively, "he will go to where the boy is."

Ahmed shrugged his shoulders again.

"When Moulay Ibrahim comes to Marrakesh there are many places where he stays. He is building a villa, I understand, a very large, important one, but it is not yet ready. He has friends. He stays with them, sometimes with one, sometimes with another."

"Then keep a watch out for when he does arrive," Bing ordered.

"I will do that, sir. My father asked me to express his regret that we can do so little for you, but were you to come to our house, poor and unimportant though it is, there would be much talk. You understand?"

"I understand," Bing said.

Ahmed salaamed and Bing ceremoniously replied. Then the youth went swiftly away, not leaving the garden through the hole in the wall through which Melina and Bing had come the night before but travelling along the wall in the opposite direction as though he wished to cover his tracks in case anyone had seen him arrive.

Bing's mouth was a hard line of disappointment.

"What are we going to do now?" Melina asked.

"God knows," Bing replied. "These people are spineless and afraid, yet one cannot blame them. Moulay Ibrahim is powerful and their King is far away."

"You are sure the child is here somewhere?" Melina inquired.

"Sure of it," Bing said positively. "Casablanca is too new a city and too French for Moulay Ibrahim to have the power and influence that he has here. No, I am convinced that he would keep to his own haunts. The difficulty is to find out where they might be."

He walked a few paces up and down the garden, then said:

"Go and sit on the steps of the temple. If anyone comes when I am away, do not speak, hold out your hands supplicatingly as if you are a beggar. I shall not be gone long and I will bring you back food and something to drink."

"I am so thirsty," Melina said, "that if you don't bring me back something I shall drink from the fountain."

"That's blackmail," Bing replied lightly, "because to have you ill at the moment would be an inconvenience that I cannot possibly afford."

"Then bring me something quickly," Melina smiled.

"Look after yourself," Bing said quietly. He looked down as he spoke into her eyes darkened by kohl. He had no idea until now how blue they were.

Just for a moment it seemed to Melina that he was about to say something of importance; and then as if he thought better of it, she merely heard him whisper half beneath his breath: "Allah take care of you, my dear!"

She wanted to reply to him, she wanted to say that it was he who must be taken care of, not her; but in a few strides he was out of earshot and she saw him push his way through the shrubs towards the hole in the wall.

It was then that she sank down on the cut grass on which they had slept together all night and prayed, not to Allah but to God to whom she had said her prayers ever since she was a child.

"Please, God, take care of him. Do not let anything happen to him and, oh God, make him love me a little."

She felt the tears trickle through her fingers with the intensity of her cry and she went on praying for a long time in the quietness and still of the garden.

10

Lileth Schuster, sitting in front of the dressing-table, scrutinised her face carefully in the mirror. The new cream she was using, although fantastically expensive, was not achieving the results she had expected.

The manufacturers' brochure had promised that wrinkles would vanish in a fortnight and that a woman's skin would look like a girl's of eighteen in a month. Lileth had conscientiously followed the instructions, but there were undoubtedly tiny wrinkles at the corners of her eyes and the hard line from her nose to her mouth was still there.

And yet she was a beautiful woman. She turned her face first this way and then the other and decided that she was lovelier now than she had been five years ago when Bing and then two millionaires, one after the other, had found her irresistible. They had not been the only men to acclaim her beauty, but they had been the only three who had interested her.

She thought of Bing and gave a deep sigh which seemed to come from the very depths of her beautifully shaped body. With a sudden gesture she pulled aside the soft nylon wrap she was wearing and stared at her nakedness with the same critical eye with which she had appraised her face.

She was remembering those long, hot nights in New York when Bing had held her closely and sworn that he would never let her go. She was remembering the wild ecstasy of their passion together and the way that her heart would beat faster at least an hour before they met in Central Park after her day's work as a stenographer had ended.

"Bing! Bing!" She could hear her voice, young and

151

tremulous, saying his name over and over again before his lips, hungry and possessive, silenced her and she was lost in a red mist of desire and unutterable joy.

Why had she been such a fool as to let him go? She knew the answer even as she asked herself the question; knew it as her hand reached out toward the gold-topped bottles from her fitted dressing-case; knew it as she saw the glitter of diamonds and rubies from her open jewelcase; knew it in the profusion of expensive dresses which hung behind her in the wardrobe.

She wanted money! God, how she'd wanted it!

"We've got each other," Bing had said to her, not once but a hundred times. And with her body quivering against his she had tried to believe it was enough; but she had known that some cold, critical part of herself stood aside and answered: "I want more."

She had hated her work as a stenographer and she had hated almost as much, although it was more interesting, her work as a model. She had changed her occupation merely because she believed, and rightly, that modelling would give her a chance to meet rich people. What she had meant, though she hardly dared put it into words even to herself, was that she would meet rich men.

She had been right. That was exactly what had happened. She could see Carl Fulton's eyes now as he had sat in the *salon* choosing a dress for his grand-daughter. She had known instinctively, as she walked towards him swaying her hips, that he was interested in her and not in the gown she was showing. Almost mechanically, as she had turned, she had glanced at him sideways under her long false eyelashes and been startled by the expression on his face.

He had meant to have her from that moment, just as he had meant to have railroads and the shipyards which had made him a millionaire long before he was thirty— nearly fifty years ago.

"I want you! You're the loveliest thing I've ever seen. What shall I give you?"

152

It was a question he had asked before with success, but even he had been surprised by Lileth's reply.

"Something very simple," she had answered. "A wedding ring!"

She had not really expected that he would agree so easily, but he was infatuated as only an old man almost in his dotage could become infatuated with a young woman.

"We will be married," he said without hesitation.

It was Lileth who had hesitated then, when she was alone and knew that she had to break the news to Bing. She had known in her heart of hearts that it was not a question of making a decision—she had already made it. But she could not help looking dispassionately at what she was doing and having a vague idea of what it was going to cost her emotionally.

Bing had come to her lodgings that night. Since they had become lovers they had given up meeting in Central Park. Instead, they grudged every moment they must spend in public away from the intimacy they could enjoy alone, the kisses which seemed so much more interesting than any conversation.

She heard Bing open the door with the latch-key she had given him and she took a last look round the tiny, sordid room for which she paid a disproportionate amount of her salary every week. She knew every lump in the hard bed, the way the wall-paper was peeling in one corner, the worn carpet, the ugly curtains which failed to hide the dirt on the windows.

She had hated the small stained bath more every time she used it. She never went into the tiny kitchenette without feeling resentful that the stove was so old and the sink needed replacing.

Just for a second she shut her eyes and saw the big, cool, pillared hall of Carl Fulton's house. She saw the Renoir hanging on the wall, the flowers which scented and decorated every room and which cost more each week than she earned in a month. She knew then that the die was cast.

"Lileth! I hadn't expected you to be home so soon."

153

Bing threw his hat on to a chair and in two strides had crossed the room and taken her in his arms.

"Darling, this is wonderful!" he cried. "I thought I should have to wait at least an hour before I saw you."

He had a small bunch of flowers in his hand and Lileth heard the paper crackle against her back as he put his arms around her, and then she shut her eyes and felt his mouth on hers, kissing her hungrily, possessively and with a sense of urgency which they both knew so well.

She wanted to stop; she wanted to tell him what had happened; but she felt as if it had suddenly become quite unimportant. The only thing that mattered was Bing's lips awakening her desire. . . .

A long time—a very long time—afterwards Lileth rose, lit a cigarette and stood looking down at the flowers Bing had brought her. They were a small, pathetic bunch of rather tired carnations. She knew he would have gone without lunch to buy them and something within her wanted to weep that such a sacrifice was necessary.

Then she remembered the orchids that Carl Fulton had given her the night before. She had hidden them in a cupboard so that Bing should not see them, but she knew that she might just as well have thrown them away because there would be more orchids every day, every hour, if she wanted them.

"We must go out to dinner," Bing murmured lazily from the bed.

"Not tonight," Lileth answered. "I've got an engagement."

Bing sat up sharply.

"What the hell do you mean, not tonight?" he asked jealously. "And what engagement? You haven't told me about it before."

"Something that has come up unexpectedly," Lileth answered.

"To do with work?"

"Not exactly."

"Then what?" Bing inquired. "You know I don't

154

allow you to go out with anyone else, if that's what you are trying to do

Lileth stubbed out her cigarette deliberately.

"It's not a question of allow, Bing," she said. "You know as well as I do that you can't afford to give me dinner, and quite frankly, I'm hungry."

He looked at her with a bewildered expression on his face.

"I don't know what you're getting at," he answered. "I've got enough money for dinner. Not at the Waldorf Astoria, but in some small place where we can be together. It's what we had planned if you remember."

"But we've got to face facts sooner or later," Lileth said. Because she was nervous her voice was unnecessarily loud.

Bing jumped to his feet and walking to her side put his hands on her shoulders and turned her round to face him.

"What's going on?" he asked. "What are you trying to tell me?"

"I'm going to be married!"

Lileth hadn't meant to blurt it out like that and when she saw his face whiten she thought that she might as well have dealt him a blow between the eyes.

"To be married!" He repeated the words stupidly.

"Yes, to Carl Fulton."

His hands dropped from her shoulders.

"The millionaire! I've heard of him, of course. Who hasn't? I had no idea you knew him."

"I've known him nearly a week."

"I see. And he actually wants to marry you. That's a break isn't it?"

The bitterness in his voice stung her.

"Oh, Bing, don't take it like that. Nothing will be altered. We can go on seeing each other. I shall never love anyone but you; but I can't go on as I am. Can't you understand? I hate this place; I hate having to work, having no money, having to walk instead of taking a taxi. I can't stand it any longer."

Bing turned his back on her and moved across the

155

room to the window. He stood breathing deeply as if the hot air was something absolutely necessary to him.

Lileth, because she was nervous, rushed into speech.

"He's old, Bing, and he wants someone to be with him—a ... a companion I think. I can keep him amused and entertained but ... but it's quite different from us. Try to understand."

He turned then and she was unable to meet the agony in his eyes.

"You're lying!" he accused. "You always have lied, but it was about things that didn't matter. You know Carl Fulton's reputation as well as I do where women are concerned. You will be his third—or is it fourth wife? He may be old and drooling, but he doesn't want a companion—he wants a woman. And he believes, as all those rich old fools do, that a young one will make him feel young again."

"It won't be like that, it won't," Lileth protested. "And we'll ..."

Bing interrupted her roughly.

"Don't you dare say it!" he stormed. "Don't you dare suggest that I should be your—your paramour, your gigolo; that I should hang on to the skirts of a rich woman who hasn't got the guts to marry me but must prostitute herself to the highest bidder."

"How can you speak to me like that?" Lileth screamed, stamping her foot and half raising her hand as if she would strike him in the face.

In answer Bing stared at her, then walked across the room and picked up his hat.

"I loved you!" he said. "God knows I loved you!"

She heard the door slam behind him.

"He'll come back," she thought, "when he's got over it."

She played with the idea of running after him, catching him before he reached the street. Then she remembered that Carl Fulton would be waiting.

The car was calling for her in a quarter-of-an-hour and she had only that time in which to have a bath and put on the dress which he had told her to buy. It was hanging at this very moment in her wardrobe, still covered with the tissue paper and the cellophane bag in which it had arrived, in case Bing should see it before she had time to break the news to him.

She had meant to do it in quite a different way, and she thought now that she ought to have been more plaintive, more pathetic about her penury. Perhaps Bing would have understood that.

Well, she would have plenty of time to make him see reason, either before the wedding or afterwards. She would ring him up first thing in the morning, but for the moment it was impossible for her to do anything but get dressed and not keep Carl Fulton waiting longer than was absolutely necessary. . . .

Lileth came back from the past to stare at her reflection in the mirror. She had never seen Bing again until the night before last at Moulay Ibrahim's party. She had not believed it possible that he would disappear out of her life.

For the first few days after he had left her lodgings she had not worried unduly. He was sulking, getting over the shock, realising that he could not have things exactly as he wanted them. He would come crawling back and apologise for making her feel anxious.

She began to plan the presents she would give him— a notecase; gold cuff-links from Cartier. She might even be able to squeeze enough money out of her very ample dress allowance to give him a car without Carl being suspicious.

But Bing had not turned up before her wedding day, and when she returned to New York after a cruise in the Caribbean in Carl's luxury yacht, which was almost like a small liner, she had been unable to find him.

She supposed now it was because he had changed his name. Cutter! How could she be expected to go about looking for a man called Cutter when his name was really Ward? And now she had found him only to discover that he was married to that tedious, inefficient ex-secretary of hers.

It seemed an almost incredible joke for fate to play.

157

But what did it matter? Divorces were easy and now that Bing was rich, they wouldn't have to go through all those tiresome exhibitions of pride which would have been inevitable if she had all the money. He would never let her pay for anything when they were together. She could imagine what scenes there would have been if she had tried to persuade him to live on Carl's millions.

She was disturbed by a sudden noise outside the window. Lileth's suite in the Mamounia Hotel overlooked the flower-filled garden. Her bedroom, with the big private sitting-room opening out of it, had wide balconies filled with comfortable chairs on which she could sit in the morning and look at the panorama of the Atlas mountains while she sipped her coffee.

The noise came again and this time Lileth rose to her feet pulling her wrap around her.

"Who is there?" she asked, in a voice which was a little apprehensive because she knew there was no question of a servant entering her room from the balcony.

It was then that a robed figure clambered swiftly over the balustrade and walking across the balcony entered the lighted room. Lileth opened her lips to shout for help and then the cry was arrested in her throat for the man in Arab dress spoke.

"Don't scream, Lileth!" he said.

"Bing!" Lileth ejaculated his name on a note of triumph. "Bing, I was thinking of you. I have been sitting here for ages just thinking of you and wondering how soon I could see you again. And now you're here. But why . . . why the fancy dress?"

In answer Bing walked quickly across the room and bolted the door from the inside, then did the same to the door opening on to the sitting-room.

"Nobody is likely to come in," Lileth said practically. "I told the maid I was going to bed early. I'm tired. I've had a long journey today."

"I know that," Bing said.

"I can't believe you are here," Lileth said, her eyes on

158

his face. "I telephoned the Jasmin Hotel yesterday and they said you'd left—you and your wife."

Her voice sharpened a little.

"That's right," Bing answered.

"Why didn't you leave a message for me?" Lileth asked.

"We had to get out in rather a hurry," Bing said.

"Don't tell me you were doing a moonlight flit?" Lileth asked with a smile. "Nowadays, with your millions, that's surely unnecessary?"

"There are other reasons for leaving quickly besides an inability to pay the bill," Bing said. "Listen, Lileth, I want your help."

"You want my help," Lileth repeated. "Oh, Bing, how wonderful! What can I do to help you? You know I'll do anything."

"Do I know that?" Bing inquired, raising his eyebrows.

Lileth had the grace to look slightly ashamed.

"Let's start at the beginning," she said hastily. "It's so long since I've seen you that I feel that while you are still Bing, still the man I have been looking for all these years, you're just a little bit of a stranger. Answer me one question first—why are you dressed like that?"

Bing hesitated and Lileth gave an exclamation and put her fingers to her lips.

"Oh, but of course, I know! How silly of me to ask. You were playing with the idea of being mixed up in the Secret Service or some such thing, even before you left me. I remember you talking about it. We were sitting in that funny little café we used to go to to have a quiet meal. You said a friend of yours had offered you a job; that it wouldn't mean much money, but it was exciting and adventurous and the sort of life you really liked."

"Yes, I remember our talking about it," Bing said quietly.

"I'd forgotten all about it until now," Lileth said. "But I remember saying: 'Love is an adventure, too,'

159

and you stopped talking about your job and talked about us."

"It's clever of you to remember so much," Bing said, and Lileth was not certain whether he was being sarcastic or not.

"I see now what happened," she went on quickly, "After you left me you took the job and that's why I couldn't find you. That's true, isn't it?"

"More or less," Bing agreed.

"You must have gone to all sorts of different parts of the world," Lileth said, "And there was I combing New York, Chicago and even London in the hope of finding you."

"You must have known I was not coming back," Bing said.

"How was I to know that?" she asked. "I thought you loved me."

To her surprise Bing threw back his head and laughed.

"Lileth, you're incorrigible! I thought perhaps you'd have grown up a little in these past years, but you're just the same."

"I don't know what you mean by that?" Lileth scowled.

"I think you do," he answered. "Experience hasn't taught you much, has it? Not about men at any rate."

"I don't know what you are talking about," Lileth replied. "I only know that I loved you, Bing, and you walked out on me. I suffered more than you could believe possible all those years."

"But comfortably, my dear, very comfortably."

Lileth gave a little sob.

"You're being beastly to me," she complained. "I made a mistake—I admit it now. I thought, as I told you at the time, that Carl Fulton wanted a companion. You were right; he wanted something very, very different. He was old and perverted and ... beastly. Even now, when he has been dead three years, I wake up screaming when I remember what I had to go through."

"But look what you got for it," Bing said quietly.

160

The gesture of his hand embraced the room, the jewel-case on the dressing-table, the white mink wrap which Lileth had carried down to dinner just in case even on a warm night she should feel cold.

"Don't let us talk of those things," Lileth pleaded. "Let us forget them—forget everything that is in the past with all the future in front of us."

Bing's lips twisted a little wryly.

"Do you really believe that?" he asked. "After six years of being apart."

"I missed you every moment of them," Lileth told him. "And I know that though you are pretending that you had forgotten me, you remembered me even as I remembered you. What could that girl to whom you're married now give you that I couldn't give you? It was only money that stood between us, and now we're both rich and it's all so easy, so very simple. Can't you understand?"

"I'm afraid the money, as far as I'm concerned, was slightly exaggerated," Bing said.

Lileth looked bewildered.

"I mean," Bing replied, "that the godfather with the oil wells was just a fairy tale invented on the spur of the moment."

"Then you're not rich?" Lileth asked.

"I'm not starving," Bing replied. "My father died several years ago and left me enough so that I never need be hungry again. But I can't measure up to your millions, Lileth."

"That wouldn't matter," Lileth said sweepingly. "I've got enough for us both—in fact far more than we shall ever spend."

"Lileth, my dear, I'm not going to spend your money. You know that quite well," Bing said. "And you've got to face facts and realise that what happened six years ago is now over—over for ever and ever."

"You mean you don't love me?" Lileth asked.

Bing shook his head.

"Not any more," he said gently.

"I don't believe it," Lileth retorted. "I just don't

161

believe it. You think you've got over me because your pride was hurt, because you wouldn't face facts and admit that it was hell for me to go on as I was. I couldn't stand poverty, Bing, it was killing me. But now everything is different. Now we can start again. We can be happy, really happy."

"Lileth, there are, I am sure, a lot of men in the world who would like you to say that to them."

"But I want only you," Lileth protested. "I have always wanted only you. I've never loved anyone but you. It may seem extraordinary but it's true. You were the man I loved and I never realised for one moment that I would have to live without you just because I wanted a few comforts, a few things that are necessities for a woman."

Bing gave a sigh as if the effort of arguing with Lileth was exhausting him.

"May I have a cigarette?" he asked.

Lileth picked up her case off the dressing-table. It was of onyx with a ruby and a diamond clasp and her initials in the same stones. Bing took a cigarette, lit it and then turned the case over and over in his fingers.

"You were the one who always said that money didn't count," Lileth said defiantly.

"Now I am older," Bing replied, "I should have added, 'to some people'."

He got to his feet and walked backwards and forwards across the room as if he were debating something. Lileth followed him for a moment with her eyes and then she rose and trailing the flowing skirts of her wrap behind her settled herself on a *chaise-longue* by the window.

The lights were less bright in this corner of the room and as her head fell back against the satin cushions she looked very seductive and extremely beautiful as she held out her hand to him.

"Come and sit near me," she said and her voice was low and inviting.

"I want to tell you why I came here," Bing said.

162

"You have already told me—to ask my help," Lileth answered.

"That's right," Bing said. "I saw you arrive tonight."

"With Moulay Ibrahim?" Lileth asked. "He's attractive, isn't he? But what counted really was that he offered to drive me down in his big Mercedes. I knew how much more comfortable it would be than travelling with Ambrose."

"You were always one for comfort, weren't you?" Bing said. "I'm quite sorry for Ambrose."

"Oh, he didn't really mind," Lileth answered. "He's under an obligation to me: I'm paying for his Art Gallery."

"And money can put everything right, can't it?" Bing asked.

"Stop it!" Lileth said almost angrily. "Stop sniping at me. Tell me how I can help you and then we can talk about ourselves."

Bing hesitated and she knew he was choosing his words.

"I am here, Lileth, as you have guessed, on a very special mission," he said. "And you can help me by telling me everything that Moulay Ibrahim said which could in any way help me to find someone he has hidden in Marrakesh."

"He was very interested in you—he had seen us dancing together," Lileth said. "But he didn't tell me anything about anyone he had hidden."

"No, of course not, but think back over everything that happened on the whole journey," Bing said. "I know what an excellent memory you have for detail. Did anyone come and speak to him? Did you hear him talking on the telephone? You must have stopped for lunch. Was there anything which, thinking back now, seemed to you unusual or perhaps a clue to what I am after?"

"It seems such a strange thing to ask," Lileth said slowly.

"Listen, Lileth, this is desperately important," Bing told her. "Someone's life depends on it—someone

163

whom I am trying to help, to rescue, if you prefer the word. Now do you understand?"

"But what has Moulay Ibrahim got to do with it?" Lileth inquired. "You're not asking me to believe that he's likely to kill someone?"

She hesitated a moment and then smiled.

"I believe he might kill. He's got a kind of brutal look about him at times. It's that which makes him so exciting."

"Think, Lileth! Think!" Bing insisted.

"I'm trying to make you jealous," Lileth said poutingly, "but you're not playing."

"I haven't got the time to play," Bing said angrily. "This is of vital importance, Lileth. When I saw you arrive with Moulay Ibrahim tonight, I was standing with a crowd of natives outside the hotel. I felt that in some extraordinary way you were the link I've been waiting for. Do you remember how you used to laugh about my intuition? How I used to know about things almost before they happened? Well, that same intuition makes me certain tonight that you can tell me what I want to know. So think! If you ever loved me, Lileth, think now!"

Lileth's eyes narrowed.

"So it's as important as all that, is it?"

"More important than I can ever explain in words," Bing said.

Lileth was silent for a moment and watching her Bing knew that she was thinking, calculating something. Then with a little glint in her eyes she said:

"Where is your wife? Does she know what this mission of yours is all about?"

"Melina is trying to help me," Bing said.

"And I shall be very surprised if she's much use," Lileth said. "You don't love her, Bing. You never have loved her, I know that."

"I don't want to discuss her," Bing said quickly.

"I wonder if you really are married?" Lileth said shrewdly. "You lied to me about your godfather and the oil wells. Perhaps you lied about Melina as well."

164

"The time is passing," Bing said desperately. "I cannot stay here; I've got things to do. Concentrate, Lileth, on what I have asked you. Nothing else is so important at the moment."

"Nothing else?" Lileth asked softly.

"Nothing else except that I should rescue this ... this person if I can find him," Bing said.

Lileth swung her feet off the *chaise-longue* and stood looking at her reflection in the mirror.

"I told you that I was thinking of you before you came here, Bing," she said softly, "I was thinking, too, that I was still beautiful and the love we had for each other would not die easily. Very well, I'll tell you what you want to know—but on my terms. Are you prepared to accept them?"

Bing, too, had risen to his feet. There was no expression on his stain-darkened face, but his eyes were suddenly alert and watchful as he answered.

"And what are your terms?"

Lileth turned round to face him and as she did so she released the sash of her wrap and the soft material swung back to reveal a glimpse of her white skin and the curves of her pointed breasts.

"My terms are very simple, Bing," she answered. "They are that you should come back to me."

Bing's eyes met hers and they stared at each other across the intervening space between them. For a moment he did not speak and then he asked:

"Do you really mean this?"

"You know that I always mean what I say," Lileth answered.

Bing did not reply and after a moment she said:

"Is the price too high for the information that I have? I'm certain that I know what you wish to hear."

"How can I be sure of that?" Bing asked almost harshly.

"It's a gamble you've got to take," Lileth said. "Well, is the answer yes or no?"

For a moment she thought she had lost and then she saw Bing capitulate.

"Tell me what you have heard," he said, "and I will come back to you—if I'm still alive!"

"Do you swear it?" Lileth insisted.

"I swear it," Bing replied.

11

Melina was becoming frightened. It was hours since Bing had left her. He had told her that he might be some time as he wanted to move around the town and see if he could hear anything which would give him a clue to where the child was being kept prisoner.

"Try not to worry," he had said. "You will be safe here and I promise you I will be back as soon as I possibly can."

It did, in fact, seem to be a safe hiding-place although it was so near the market-place. The only visitors had been a few small children and when they had seen Bing and Melina sitting on the steps of the tomb they had run away as if they knew they were doing wrong in encroaching on sacred ground.

The sun was still high when Bing left and Melina lay in the shadow of the trees and listened to the birds chirping above her and wondered if any other girl had ever found herself in a more extraordinary predicament or taken part in a more fantastic adventure.

How little she had guessed when she took the job with Mrs. Schuster that this would be the outcome. How little she had thought then that the adventure would not only bring her the thrill of excitement, but love.

She knew now that she was falling more deeply in love with Bing every moment. It was hard not to show him how much she loved him, not only by the expression in her eyes when she looked at him, but in her longing to touch him, to cling to him when he left her, to run towards him with a joy that was beyond an indication of relief when he returned.

Twilight came swiftly, then the darkness; and as the

moon began to climb the skies Melina decided that she would do something which she had been longing to do ever since they first came to the garden. She would have a proper wash.

She slipped off her clothes and got into the little, broken fountain where she had washed bit by bit, and felt the pleasure of the cool water on her hot body and the joy of being clean after the dust and the sticky heat of the djellabah.

She didn't dare linger over her bathe, knowing that Bing might be back at any moment, and apart from the fact of her not wishing him to see her naked she had the idea that he would be annoyed at her taking such a risk.

She just had time to rub herself clean and then to run to the shadow of a tree where she had left her clothes before she thought she heard someone coming. It was a false alarm—it must have been a cat or a stray dog rummaging its way through the bushes but it was enough to make Melina scurry into her clothes and pull the djellabah quickly over her head. Then, as she waited apprehensively, the movement was gone and there was only the silence.

She took her time, therefore, to stroll across the garden and back to the comfortable mound of grass which they had used as a mattress. There was a little stack of food on one side of it which Bing had brought earlier in the day. There was also fruit and several bottles of mineral water—rather unpleasant and gassy but which he had told her was the only thing he could buy except an Arab version of Coca-Cola.

Melina was not hungry; she was only waiting and hoping with every nerve of her body for Bing's return.

"I love him!"

She whispered the words and felt they were an expression of love such as no one had ever given before.

"I love him!"

How simple it was to say that and how difficult in reality to face the fact that though she loved him he did not love her. Did he really still want Lileth Schuster?

168

She was beautiful, Melina thought with a stab of jealousy; beautiful and charming enough where any man was concerned. It was only that she had been in a position to see beneath the surface and know how hard and tyrannical those lovely eyes could be and how sharp the tongue which would only utter honeyed words when there was anyone of importance about.

"Oh Bing! Bing! She'll hurt you! She'll break your heart!" she whispered to the trees, and thought that her love was great enough for her to give him up if she believed it meant his happiness—but not to someone like Lileth Schuster.

The hours went by and still Bing did not come. Now Melina began to feel afraid. Supposing something had happened to him? Supposing he made some wild, crazy attempt to rescue the child by himself, and had failed? Supposing he was Moulay Ibrahim's prisoner or, worse still, killed or injured by one of the guards?

How would she ever learn what had happened to him and what should she do herself? She saw herself waiting and waiting all through the night and perhaps all through tomorrow before she would be forced to find some British person—perhaps a Consul or someone in authority—to whom she could tell her incredible story.

Was it likely they would believe her? Bing was working on his own: he had said that often enough. Would anyone credit that an English girl, sacked from one job, would entertain the possibility of another in which she pretended to be a stranger's wife and found herself abandoned in a ruined garden, dressed in a djellabah and a very dilapidated evening dress? It would be funny, Melina thought, if it wasn't so frightening.

She got to her feet and tried to peer through the bushes which bordered the broken wall. She dared not push her way through them for that might draw attention to herself and would be, indeed, madness; but she could see nothing and hear nothing except the very distant sounds from Djemaa El Fna.

169

Miserably she went back to the improvised bed and sat there playing a game she had played as a child.

"I will count fifty and then he will come."

She had counted slowly and deliberately, lingering over each number so as to spin it out.

"I will count one hundred . . ."

"I will count five hundred . . ."

Actually he came when she had reached four hundred and thirty-two, and just for a moment, because she was afraid she thought it was not Bing but a stranger. A man came through the bushes and stood in the moonlight and Melina drew a deep breath. And then she saw it was Bing and ran towards him.

"Bing! Bing! I thought you were never coming!"

The djellabah fell back from her head as she ran and as she reached him she put out her arms in sheer gladness as she flung herself against him, her head with its halo of red-gold curls vivid in the moonlight, her face turned up to his, her lips parted in excitement.

"I have been so frightened that something had happened to you. But you are here! Thank God you are here!"

Without thinking what she did she pulled him close to her and then his arms went round her and he held her suddenly with a strength and a passion which checked the words as they flowed from her mouth.

For a moment her eyes were wide with surprise and then his lips were on hers, kissing her hungrily, greedily, and with a fierceness that she had never known—never dreamt he would show.

It seemed to her that his kisses were desperate and yet she could not analyse them. She could, after her first astonishment at his violence, be aware only of the leaping flame within her body as without her conscious volition she responded to his kisses with a wildness that equalled his own.

It was as if the world spun around them. She knew nothing save that Bing was kissing her and that she loved him. She was beyond thought, only aware of the glorious breathless feeling within her throat, the throbbing of her heart, the sudden heaviness of desire which seemed to close her eyes. She wanted him to go on kissing her forever and she felt as if time stood still because he was doing so.

And then abruptly, almost as fiercely as he had taken her in his arms, Bing set her aside. He pushed her from him so that she stumbled and almost fell. He walked away from her and stood with his back to her without speaking.

Then he took a handkerchief from inside his native robe and wiped his forehead.

"You go to a man's head, Melina," he said in a queer, strangled voice that she didn't understand.

"Bing! Oh, Bing!"

She hardly breathed his name and, in a tone that was suddenly harsh, he said:

"There's no time to talk of anything now but our plans. I have a lot to tell you. Come over here."

He walked away without waiting for her, towards the grass mound. Melina watched him go. There was a singing in her ears and she felt as if her whole body tingled at the miracle of his kiss.

It was with an effort that she remembered the child; the reason they were here; Bing's mission; the danger in which they stood. Did any of it matter, she longed to ask, beside the fact that she loved him and, because he had kissed her in such a manner, he must love her?

"Melina!"

He called her across the garden and his voice was sharp.

"I'm coming!"

She forced herself to speak ordinarily, to come down from the clouds to the firm earth below. Bing had work to do. Their personal lives could not intrude upon it until it was completed. She understood that. She must force herself to help him, to do nothing which might in any way seem an obstacle in the path of duty.

Feeling as if her legs had turned to cotton-wool, conscious that her lips were burning, Melina walked

171

across the moonlit space to the shadows of the trees where they had made their little home.

Bing was already seated on the grass, his arms clasping his knees. He did not look up as she arrived, but stared ahead of him as if he was concentrating fiercely, so that she dropped on her knees beside him and said nothing for a minute or so, not daring to interrupt.

"I know where the child is!" he said at length, and it seemed to her that there was some strange undercurrent of feeling in his voice, but ostensibly his tone was hard, brusque and businesslike.

"You've found him!" Melina breathed. "How wonderful! Where is he?"

"In the House of the Doves," Bing answered. "It's a large, rambling, native house that was once the palace of an important family who have gradually died out. There's only one old man living there and he's ill. It's a clever place to choose because no one in Marrakesh would connect the house in any way with Moulay Ibrahim."

"He is staying there too?" Melina said.

Bing shook his head.

"No, he is too clever for that. He is staying at the Mamounia Hotel. He has a large suite there and will doubtless be entertaining a number of friends and politicians. It's a perfect cover for his own activities."

"Is the child guarded?" Melina asked.

"Naturally," Bing answered sharply, as if impatient at her question. "Moulay Ibrahim has seen to that."

"Then what are we going to do?"

"I have thought of a plan and I have already discussed it with Ahmed and his family," Bing replied. "There's one chance in a million that we can pull it off, so it is desperately dangerous."

He was silent again and after a second or two Melina ventured to say timidly:

"Aren't you going to tell me about the plan?"

"I'm going to tell you," Bing said, "and then ask you whether you will help me or whether you won't."

"I can answer that now," she said eagerly.

172

He held up his hand to stop her.

"Wait!" he said. "You haven't heard yet what it is."

Because she recognised by the serious tone of his voice that this was not a moment for her to make protestations of fidelity Melina was silent.

"The house is in the native quarter of the town," Bing started. "It is a large building but the only entrance is through an opening off a narrow street. The gateway leads into a courtyard on the right-hand side of which are kitchens."

"Yes," Melina prompted, wondering why he was troubling to explain all this to her.

"I went with Ahmed to have a look at the gateway," Bing continued. "There are two guards standing at the door and at night the place is barred and bolted and it would be impossible for anyone to get in. The only chance is in the day-time when the doors are open to allow the servants and those who deliver food to enter."

"But the guards?" Melina questioned.

"They are there and they carry weapons beneath their cloaks," Bing said dryly.

It appeared to Melina an almost impossible task to get past them, but she knew that Bing had some plan and therefore she was silent until he continued:

"Ahmed knows the baker who brings the freshly baked bread each morning. He calls there and his wife accompanies him, carrying live chickens for the cook who wants five or six every day."

Bing's voice died away and Melina began to see what he was trying to tell her.

"You mean that we should go instead of the baker and his wife?" she said.

"The baker has agreed," Bing answered, "because he is hard up and his elder daughter wishes to get married. It's a great risk on his part, but the money tempted him."

"And once we get in . . ." Melina began.

"We haven't got as far as that yet," Bing answered. "I could go alone—which I should prefer to do—but

173

the baker tells me that he is always accompanied by his wife, and the guards, who are local men and who always watch the door, not merely because there is an extra visitor in the house, might ask questions if she did not appear."

"But why should a man who is ill want guards?" Melina asked out of curiosity.

"Because he is very rich and it gives him a sense of self-importance," Bing replied. "These minor sheiks and local princes like to think they have their own private army. Moulay Ibrahim had been wise enough to turn that to his own advantage."

"Yes, of course, I see," Melina murmured.

"I would much prefer not to take you, but I want every thing to appear commonplace and ordinary," Bing went on. "This is no joking matter, Melina. It's going to be an extremely dangerous and difficult operation to get inside the house and to rescue the boy. I may fail utterly, in which case it will be very unlikely that I shall come out alive. They might spare your life, as a woman, but it isn't a thing that one would care to insure against."

"I'm coming with you," Melina said firmly. "There's no question for me to answer, Bing, I'm coming with you. I'll see this adventure through and if we die, we die."

She saw in the moonlight the expression on Bing's face as he turned towards her and took her hand in his.

"Thank you, darling," he said softly. "I somehow knew you'd say that."

She felt herself tremble at the touch of his hand and the note in his voice as he called her "darling" for the first time. Then her hand was free and Bing had resumed the hard, brusque tone in which he had started to speak of his plans.

"I hate to think I have brought you into this," he said. "But if we are going to do it, we will do everything in our power to try and succeed. Ahmed is coming in the morning at five o'clock. There are not many hours ahead of us. We have got to sleep. We shall need

174

all our intelligence if we are to come out of this alive, so sleep, relax, so that our minds will be active and we do not lose all we have gained by being slow brained."

He might have been giving a lecture to a number of students, Melina thought, but she was too happy to criticise him. He had kissed her and that was enough. He loved her a little, she was sure of that now, and her whole heart was overflowing with gratitude.

"Sleep!" he commanded and flung himself down on the grass and pulled his native robe around him.

Meekly Melina settled herself beside him. He was not asleep, she knew that; he was not even relaxed. She could feel it by the tenseness of his body. But because he wished to pretend that he was already unconscious she pretended too, shutting her eyes, trying to breathe quietly, and feeling the thrill of happiness run through her because he was so near and she had only to put out her hand to touch him.

She must have dozed a little during the hours of darkness but she was too happy to sleep and she was well aware that Bing was not asleep either. She wished she could believe that he was thinking of her, but she knew he was thinking of only one thing—the rescue of the child.

Finally she fell into a fitful slumber, only to feel Bing's hand touch her shoulder and his voice say quietly, in little above a whisper:

"Ahmed has come!"

She sat up quickly to see Ahmed walking across the garden as the first golden fingers of the sun shot across the sky. He was followed by another man, older and rather bowed, who Melina guessed at once was his father.

The older man salaamed with the exquisite courtesy of his generation and Bing returned his greeting. Then they settled themselves cross-legged on the grass and produced a small bundle of things which Bing needed for his disguise as the baker.

Fortunately the man wore glasses and had, as Bing explained to Melina, a rather nondescript face without any distinctive features. He had, also, Ahmed told them, suffered from boils during the winter and so they put a dressing on Bing's jaw as if it concealed a sudden skin eruption.

The clothes of the baker, traditional to all the Moslem world, were soon assumed and with a little makeup round his eyes, which Ahmed applied with a skillful hand, Bing looked very unlike himself and Ahmed stood back with a cry of delight.

"It is Seddig! he exclaimed. "Not even the mother who bore him would know it was not her son. You must walk as he does, sir, with a slight limp, for Seddig was kicked by his mule last year and always he tells the story of the animal's ingratitude and how never again will he own a creature on four legs."

"I noticed his limp yesterday," Bing said. "Is this how he walks?"

He walked away from them across the garden and Ahmed and his father clapped their hands together.

"It is excellent, sir, but the head on one side a little more," said the old man. "Remember the boil on your chin is hurting."

"And now Seddig's wife! What does she look like?" Bing asked.

The eyes of all three men were on Melina.

"I have not looked at her," the old man said with dignity, "but the guards are often impudent creatures of the young generation."

He gave a sidelong glance at his son as he spoke.

"There is no reason why they should look closely at this hour of the morning," Ahmed suggested.

"You have brought the thicker yashmak?" Bing inquired.

"I have done so sir."

He brought out a yashmak of thick, black gauze such as the more strict women of the Moslem faith assume. He handed it to Melina who took it, wondering as she did so how any woman could tolerate such coarse material in the heat.

176

"Kohl!" Bing exclaimed abruptly. "You have brought some more kohl?"

A small bottle was produced and he made Melina sit on the ground while he knelt beside her.

"Shut your eyes," he commanded, and she felt the soft camel-hair brush drawing the long black lines over her closed eyelids.

"Now open your eyes and look up," Bing said, and she obeyed him feeling her heart quicken because his face was so near to hers.

The brush tickled; Bing's hand was steady and she forced herself not to blink as he drew the dark line along the bottom lid and pointed it at the corners.

"Has the baker's wife blue eyes?" he inquired.

Ahmed and his father both shook their heads.

"We have no idea."

"You must keep your eyes lowered," Bing said to Melina. "And I think it would be best," he added, "to darken the top of your nose a little and what can be seen of your cheeks. The dark powder will do."

Ahmed had brought that too and when Melina had adjusted her yashmak Bing stood back at a distance.

"You'll pass," he said. "Let us hope the guards of the older generation are on today and not 'Peeping Toms'."

"I believe in emancipation and that women should discard their veils," Ahmed said defiantly.

"Such wickedness!" his father muttered. "Do not listen to him, sir. Bad devils are inside him."

"My Father thinks all modern progress is the work of the devil," Ahmed scoffed.

As if he was not interested in their personal disputes Bing turned to the older man, thanked him courteously in Arabic for all he had done, and asked that Ahmed should now lead them to the baker's shop.

"I will take you a round-about way where we will see few people," Ahmed promised. "You just follow me, sir, but we will not talk. I will walk a few paces in front and no one need know that we are even acquainted."

177

Melina could not help feeling that Ahmed was taking good care not to be involved more than necessary.

Bing turned to the older man.

"The car will be where we arranged?" he asked.

"It will be attended to," Ahmed's father replied. "Allah go with you!"

There was a sudden throb of sincerity in the words which told Melina that he, at least, was wholeheartedly on their side. And then there was no time to think of anything but that they must follow Ahmed from the safety of the garden into the dangers of the streets outside.

It was still very early but in Djemaa El Fna there was already activity. The sweepers were cleaning the streets and brushing down the wide, paved square, and the water carriers from the Atlas mountains, with their brilliantly coloured hats, were moving amongst the stall-holders offering water from bottles made from the skins of goats.

The stalls were opening up. There was the smell of cooking fat, of mint tea and also of the heat to come later in the day. Herds of goats were being driven through the streets to where, outside the city, they would find a meagre meal amongst the weeds which grew on the sandy ground despite the strength of the sun. There was the clatter of horses' hoofs and the shrill hooting of cars driven by natives who keep their fingers permanently on the horn.

It was difficult for Melina to have more than a fleeting glance at everything before she lowered her eyes and pulling her djellabah well forward over her face followed meekly behind Bing. He was moving quickly along but limping as he did so and she knew that he had already slipped into the character of the baker and assumed his personality completely.

Melina remembered that many years ago her father had said: "The perfect disguise is to think you are the person you pretend to be. It's thoughts that count far more than any trappings one can assume."

Melina knew that now Bing was thinking himself

into being the baker and she tried to think herself into the part of the baker's wife.

How happy she would be, she thought, if Bing was the baker and she could be, in fact, his wife. She imagined them living in the native town and baking bread and carrying it round to their customers, as they were pretending to do today.

Would life really be sufficient for her under those circumstances? she wondered, and knew with a little stab of her heart that even if she were content Bing would not be. He belonged not only to the world of excitement and adventure, but to the world of intelligence, the world where men were prepared to fight for what they believed to be right and true.

She saw little of the narrow street and passages through which Ahmed led them, twisting this way and then that until finally they came to a standstill and from the smell of warm bread Melina knew they had arrived.

They passed through the doorway of the shop. The room in which they found themselves was little more than a cave and on the table was a board stacked high with a great pile of flat thick loaves of unrisen bread which the natives ate and which was half covered with a white cloth. Beside it, on the table, was a large, roughly constructed reed crate. Inside, chirping and scratching against the sides, were half-a-dozen small, live chickens.

Bing shut the door behind them and now the light came into the small room only from another open door which led into a courtyard beyond.

"Seddig is hiding, sir, as you commanded," Ahmed said. "It would not be good for anyone to see two bakers this morning."

"That is what I asked," Bing approved.

"And this is all you required?" Ahmed asked, looking down at the board of bread and the basket with the chickens.

Bing lifted up the board.

"It is heavy," he exclaimed, and turned to Melina. "I

was going to ask you to carry this on your head," he said, "but I see that I shall have to do that. Can you manage the chickens, do you think?"

He stopped and a look of utter consternation came over his face.

"Fool that I am!" he cried. "Can you balance anything on your head?"

"As a matter of fact I can," Melina answered. "I went to a school where they made us walk with books on our heads for good deportment."

"You can, of course, hold the basket with one hand," Bing said. "In fact you'll want to do that. But I had not thought that your arm will show and a married woman of your standing would be wearing a gold bangle."

Ahmed held out his hand.

"Ten shillings, sir, and I find you a gold bangle such as a princess might envy."

"No!" Bing said sharply. "Do not go into the market-place. Go and find the baker's wife and buy one of hers."

He brought out a little collection of Moroccan notes and gave them to Ahmed who disappeared through the open door into the courtyard.

"I thought I had remembered everything," Bing said. "It just shows how stupid one can be. You're certain you can balance this on your head?"

"Quite certain," Melina answered. "And if I can hold it with one hand it will be quite easy. I really have learned to walk and carry things on my head—not only at school, but I used to practise with the water bottles my father had in his collection. It amused him to see if I could go upstairs without touching what I carried and only once did I break anything."

"How lucky I am to have found you," Bing murmured.

Just for a moment Melina thought that his tone changed from swift urgency to something else and his eyes, behind the ugly, steel-rimmed spectacles, softened. Then Ahmed came hurrying into the room.

"Here you are, sir. She was delighted. Tomorrow she will buy a new one—perhaps two—for what you have given her."

"That is good," Bing replied, and taking the gold bracelet from Ahmed's hand he slipped it on to Melina's wrist.

"It is fortunate that you are tiny," he said as he did so. "Few European women could squeeze their hands through a native bracelet."

He opened the chicken crate and said to Melina:

"Now, listen to me carefully. When we get through the kitchens you follow me up the stairs and the moment I am engaged with the guard, who I expect will be outside the boy's room, you enter, tell the child—in French—that you are to take him to his mother, and persuade him to lie down in this basket. If he curls himself up with his knees beneath his chin he can manage it. It has been chosen for that very purpose. I will then take the crate from you, carry it downstairs and put it on my head. You will pick up the board that I have left on the kitchen table and follow me."

"But the servants?" Melina asked.

"Everything depends on what they do, of course," Bing answered. "But I think they will do nothing."

Melina gave a little sigh. She felt somehow that Bing should have told her all this before. She thought that perhaps he had his reasons for doing everything at the last minute. She glanced at him quickly and wondered if it was because he thought that she might be too afraid to undertake the task if she had time to think it over.

"Now, do you understand?" Bing asked impatiently. "You know what to do? I may, of course, have to alter everything at the last moment. We do not know. We can only improvise as we go along. Now, put this on your head."

He lifted the crate with the chickens as he spoke and balanced it carefully. It was not heavy and putting up her hand to steady the crate, Melina realised that it would be no effort to carry it quite a long distance.

Then Bing picked up the heavily laden board, tossed the cloth over it and placed it on his own head. Ahmed opened the door; they both had to steady their burdens as they passed under the lintel and then they straightened themselves in the street.

"First to the left, sir," Ahmed murmured, "and then right."

Bing did not answer him, but Melina, without looking knew that Ahmed had now disappeared and was hurrying from the scene as quickly as he could go.

"What a coward he is," she thought scornfully, and then realised that men like Ahmed and Rasmin had everything to lose by getting involved in the wrong political faction. It was better to remain neutral as far as the ordinary man was concerned, until one side or another came out on top.

The narrow street was not long. Bing turned the corner and Melina followed him. She was proud to find how well she could walk carrying the crate. It was not half as difficult as the water bottles she had practised with or the books they were made to carry at school.

The only difficulty was when the chickens moved nervously; but after a few, frightened squawks because of the movement, they had now settled down and were crouching almost in the centre of the crate as if they realised it was the most secure place to be.

Left, now right. The street was much broader and there were more people moving along. Melina kept her eyes lowered. She could see Bing's white robes ahead of her; she could see his feet, although he was limping, moving at quite a good pace over the cobbled road.

Then, almost without looking, she realised they were there. It was a wide, arched doorway and two men were lounging, one on either side of it. One of them was smoking; the other was cleaning his knife—a long, evil-looking weapon.

They neither of them spoke and Bing and Melina passed them. They went on with what they were doing. Melina wondered why they did not hear the sudden thumping terror of her heart.

Bing crossed the courtyard. There was a bleat from a goat which was tethered to a post at the far end, but otherwise the place seemed deserted save for an ancient dog sleeping in the sun.

Bing veered to the right. There was an open door through which Melina could hear the sound of voices. Now came the real test, she thought. A sudden scream and the guards would be there; one already had a dagger in his hand.

She wondered what Bing was going to do, what he was going to say. She saw him bow his head and move the tray of bread in dexterously through the doorway. She steadied her crate of chickens with her gold-bangled arm and then she, too, was inside.

There were half-a-dozen servants in the low-ceilinged kitchen, working at a chopping-board or over the fire or washing up in a rough, wooden sink. Bing put the board down on the table and an elderly man whom Melina suspected was the chief cook wished him good morning in Arabic.

Bing replied in a low voice and taking the reed crate from Melina, put it on the table and opening it took out the chickens by their legs. The cook took them, one by one, pinching their bodies as he did so and grumbling that they were not fat enough and wondering how he was going to make a meal of them.

Melina did not understand in actual words what he said but his meaning was obvious from the gestures of his hands and his tone was the tone of every cook the world over who is confronted with food which he does not really consider up to his standard of cooking.

It was then that Bing closed the crate and gave it to Melina. Then he drew something from his pocket, held it in his hand and spoke five words:

"By the Hand of Fatima!"

There was a sudden gasp and everyone in the kitchen turned to look. He held out the jewelled hand which Rasmin had given him. It hung sparkling in the light from the window so that they could all see it.

183

"By the Hand of Fatima," Bing repeated. "I ask your silence. Say nothing; do nothing; see nothing."

They stared at him, but none of the servants screamed. Then he opened the door at the far end of the kitchen and followed by Melina started to move swiftly down a long passage. Melina felt as if she must force her legs to follow him, expecting to hear a scream and to find the guards pounding after them. But there was only silence!

Bing seemed to know his way without hesitation and she guessed that Ahmed or his father had given him a shrewd idea of the layout of the house. There was a narrow staircase and they climbed it to the first floor. Just for a moment Bing paused and as he did so they heard a child's voice cry out in French:

"Do not touch me! Leave me alone! Do not . . . hit me again I . . . pray you!"

Bing was at the door from where the cry came in two strides. He pulled it open and Melina saw over his shoulder a man with his back to them, his arm raised, a thin, narrow whip in his hand.

Bing sprang before the man could turn round. His hand was over his mouth, his other arm across his neck and he was bending him backwards . . . backwards, until his neck must break. She had a quick impression of Bing's face as she had seen it once before—the face of the devil!

But she did not look, she ran to the child who was standing against the wall, the tears running down his face. She put her arms round him and held him close.

"Do not cry," she said in French. "It is all right. I am taking you to your mama."

"To Mama, now?"

She felt the excitement run through his thin little body.

"Yes, yes, but you must be very quiet. You must not breathe. We have got to escape from this place. Will you hide in this basket?"

Only a child who had known danger and understood it, Melina thought, could have reacted so quickly. The

184

little boy did not murmur. He got into the basket which Melina opened on the floor beside him.

"Lie down," she prompted, and even as she said the words she heard a dull thump behind her and knew that Bing had killed the guard.

She tried not to think of it, to remember only the child and the tears on his face.

"Quickly! Quickly!" she said.

He obeyed her, lying down; and now Bing was at their side speaking, in French, soothing, commanding words which the little boy seemed only too ready to obey.

He picked up the crate, carrying it sideways so that the child was on his back. And then he was moving down the stairs and Melina was following him, having first shut the door, leaving the dead guard inside.

They hurried down the passage into the kitchen. Melina was terrified that they would find the outside guards waiting for them, but instead the kitchen was empty. There was no one there. The servants had all gone.

Bing pointed to the board on the table.

"Put it on your head," he said.

He lifted the child in the crate carefully on to his own head.

"Don't hurry," he whispered. "Take it easily."

Melina drew a deep breath. They were out in the sunshine. The dog was still lying in the courtyard only raising a lazy leg to scratch himself. The goat was still bleating in the distance.

She hardly dared to glance towards the guards but when she did so they were still there. The sunlight was glinting on the knife; the other man was lighting a cigarette. The man with the knife glanced up. He said something which sounded rude although perhaps it was intended as a joke. Bing bade him good-day in Arabic and then they were through the arched doorway, moving down the broad street.

They turned to the left and then, still moving without undue effort, they reached another and wider street.

There an open car was waiting. Bing laid the crate with the child on the back seat. He opened the door for Melina and then stepped into the driver's seat.

If there was anyone in attendance they did not see them, but for the moment Melina was concerned only in their not being followed. A man rounded the corner in the direction from which they had come and her heart gave a sudden leap of fear, but it was only a native moving about his own business.

Bing started up the engine. Now they were moving slowly down the street, passing water carriers and men bringing in piles of merchandise to the market stalls. They had reached the Djemaa El Fna.

Bing started to hoot his horn, to drive more quickly. They passed the gardens where they had sheltered for what seemed to Melina an aeon of time. Now they had left the market-place and the native houses behind and were in the broader and less populated streets with better class houses.

"We've done it!" Melina cried. "We've done it! Oh, Bing! We've done it!"

"Not quite yet," he answered. "Get the child out of the crate and let him sit beside us. You'll have to do it while we're moving. I can't stop."

As he spoke he put his foot on the accelerator and the car leapt forward.

12

The little boy nestled close to Melina when she put her arm round him.

"You are all right now," she told him in French. "We are taking you to your mother and father."

"Those men were bad, very bad!" he answered in a high, childish voice. "They beat me and said that tomorrow they were going to kill me."

Melina glanced over his head towards Bing who was concentrating on getting every ounce of speed out of the car.

"Do you hear that?" she asked in English. "Tomorrow! We were only just in time."

"I knew that," he answered briefly, and she wondered why he had kept the knowledge to himself and not let her share the anxiety as to how quickly the sands were running out.

"I was brave," the small boy went on. "I cried a lot, I . . . I couldn't help it, but I knew Papa would send soldiers to rescue me."

He looked up at Melina and then at Bing.

"You're not soldiers, are you?" he asked and his voice was disappointed.

"It's more exciting being rescued this way," Melina said consolingly. "And you were a very brave boy to jump into the chicken crate so quickly without arguing. If you hadn't done that, we might never have got you away."

"I was frightened at being on top of his head," the child answered, pointing at Bing.

"What is your name?" Melina asked, thinking it a mistake to go on talking about the danger that was past.

"My name is Mohammed," he answered. "Papa says

all eldest sons are called Mohammed. But Mama calls me Suki."

"I shall call you Suki then," Melina smiled, "because it's much easier to say than Mohammed. Now, Suki, why don't you go to sleep? We've got a long journey ahead of us and you will want to feel well and not tired when you reach your Mama."

"I'll try," the little boy said obediently, snuggling himself closer against Melina and shutting his eyes.

She looked down at his small, dark head and thought how gentle and confiding he was. Children were so vulnerable and she could hardly bear to think of what he had suffered and what he must have gone through in the hands of those brutes.

She was glad now that Bing had killed the guard who was whipping him. She had thought when Bing killed the man who had jumped at him from the tree in Tangier that she could never bear to look in his face again and see that expression of revenge and triumph which resulted in what she termed to herself as "the expression of the Devil."

But now she knew she was no longer afraid. What Bing had done was right in the circumstances, however much one might condemn it on ethical grounds. If they had not rescued the boy today, he would have died tomorrow; and nothing could be more horrible, more bestial, than the sacrifice of a small, innocent child for political interests.

She looked at Bing's profile and thought with a sudden melting of her heart how magnificent he had been over all this. No one else would have attempted such an operation without official support, and only someone like Bing, she thought, would have been successful.

The car was moving at what seemed to be a very fast pace down the long, straight road which stretched interminably into the distance. But she realised that other cars, particularly Moulay Ibrahim's, could go quicker, and she wondered how long it would be before the dead guard was found and Moulay Ibrahim was informed of what had happened.

She wanted to question Bing, but she knew that not only would he be impatient at having to answer her, but also that it was very difficult to talk at the speed at which they were travelling.

There was a certain amount of traffic on the road but not much. However, there were, moving along on the caravan tracks which ran parallel with the modern tarmac road, numbers of families travelling in their traditional fashion with camels and goats, mules and donkeys—the men sitting high on the backs of their animals, the women and children walking beside them.

They must have gone about ninety kilometres when the road began to descend into a valley. When they were half-way down it they saw a man in a white robe standing in the middle of the road waving his arm wildly.

"Get the child on the floor," Bing said tersely, "and cover him up."

Hastily and without argument Melina did as she was told, covering him with her djellabah, for she had nothing else, and whispering to him to keep quiet.

"What's . . . happening?" Suki asked sleepily.

"You have got to hide for a moment or two," Melina replied. "Do not speak; do not move. I am going to cover you up so no one will see you."

The child was acquiescent and obedient and she raised her head to see that they were approaching the gesticulating man and in a few seconds would be past him. Bing slowed down a little and with a little start, Melina realised that he was driving with his left hand while in his right he held a small revolver.

"If anything happens get your head down and then crouch down on the floor," Bing said quickly.

A moment later, because they were still travelling at a fast speed, the man in white was stepping out of the way to let them pass.

"By the Hand of Fatima!" he shouted and Bing jammed on the brakes.

Only by putting both her hands quickly on to the

189

dashboard did Melina save herself from being thrown against the windscreen. Bing turned his head, the revolver still in his hand, as the man came running up.

"By the Hand of Fatima, sir," he repeated. "I was waiting for you."

"How do you know who we are?" Bing asked sharply.

"My cousin, Ahmed, telephoned me," the man replied. "But a quarter of an hour ago my brother also received a telephone message. We are a house divided, sir. He is one of Moulay Ibrahim's men."

Bing slowly put his revolver back into his pocket.

"They are waiting for us?" he asked.

The man pointed ahead.

"Down there, sir, in the village. There are about ten of them."

"What is the name of this village?" Bing asked.

"El-Guelb," the man replied. "But not all, like my brother, follow Moulay Ibrahim. Many are loyal, as I am, to the King."

"Is there any other road?" Bing asked.

"There is a track, sir. It is rough and meant for camels but if you will allow me to direct you . . ."

"Jump in behind," Bing commanded him, "and show me where I turn off."

The man scrambled into the back of the car. Bing looked at his watch.

"We have been about an hour on the journey," he said to Melina in English. "If Moulay Ibrahim telephoned about a quarter of an hour ago, that means we have got nearly three-quarters of an hour's start."

"Will it be long enough?" Melina asked.

"That remains to be seen," Bing answered enigmatically.

The track was rough and it was impossible to travel at any speed. They were forced to drive inland two or three kilometres before they swung round in a circle so as to return to the main road. Several other men joined them who swore, either in Arabic or in a mixture of

French and English, that they were loyal to the King and ready to help in any way possible.

Nearly twenty minutes must have passed before they finally came back on to the main road and a signpost told them they were one hundred and forty-nine kilometres from Casablanca.

Bing thanked the first man who had said he was Ahmed's cousin.

"Delay Moulav Ibrahim if you can," he said. "A puncture if possible—anything so long as we have time to reach Casablanca before he catches up with us."

"I understand, sir," Ahmed's cousin said, grinning as if it was all a huge joke.

Amid cries of good wishes and a great waving of hands Bing manœuvred the car on to the road and they were off again. Now he seemed to crouch over the wheel, coaxing the engine into a performance that it had never dreamed of giving when it had been made.

Suki climbed up beside Melina again and seemed content to half-doze in her arms, occasionally asking plaintively how long it would be before he saw his Papa and Mama.

On . . . on . . . they went! Melina kept turning her head expecting to see a great Mercedes roaring down upon them; but there appeared to be nothing behind save the cars they passed.

She felt somehow as if they would go on driving like this for all eternity—the desert on either side of them; the sudden glimpses of farms; the occasional modern house; small villages through which they rushed with a complete disregard for traffic regulations. And then they were on and on again along the straight, modern road leading to the coast. . . .

When finally they reached the outskirts of Casablanca, Melina could hardly believe that their destination was really in sight. She wanted to cry out once again that they had done it, but something in the set of Bing's grim mouth and steady concentration of his eyes told her that he did not wish to talk.

There was still a chance that they might be stopped:

still a chance that victory might be snatched from them at the eleventh hour.

They swung away from the town and now Melina saw a notice as they flashed past and knew where they were going—the airport! Even as she realised their intention there was a sudden sound of racing engines and she saw that two motor-bicyclists wearing Army uniform had come up alongside them. For a moment she questioned whether they were friend or foe; then she saw the salute they gave Bing and realised they were, indeed, friends.

She felt some of the tension leave her as she saw the motor-bicyclists forge ahead. A gate of the Airport marked *No Admittance* was swung open and they were on the landing ground and travelling, still at great speed, down a runway.

Suddenly Melina saw ahead the great, silver wings of an airliner and the magic letters, "B.E.A." In a few seconds the car drew to a standstill. A distinguished man wearing European clothes broke away from a number of attendants—soldiers and aides-de-camp— and ran forward. The tears were running down his face as he took Bing's hand in his then held out his arms to Suki.

"Papa! Papa!" the small boy screamed, scrambling over Melina's lap to kiss his father.

He picked up the child in his arms and apparently incapable of words carried him, almost running, towards the aeroplane. A woman, obviously a Moroccan but dressed in the latest Parisian fashion, was standing at the top of the gangway.

She, too, was weeping as the small boy scrambled up the steps and rushed into her arms. They turned and waved to the man waiting below, then the steps were wheeled away, the door of the liner was slammed to and the aeroplane started to taxi down the runway.

Only as it moved off Melina with tears in her eyes, turned from looking at this moving, human drama towards Bing. He was lying back against the driving seat and for a moment he looked utterly and completely exhausted. His hands were limp at his sides and they, perhaps more than any thing else, told her of the nervous tension he had been through in the last twenty-four hours.

But as Suki's father came hurrying towards the car, Bing got out and went to meet him.

"Two minutes more and the plane would have gone," he said, the words coming almost incoherently between his lips. "They held it for twenty minutes; they would not have been able to do so any longer."

The tears were still running down his cheeks and he pulled himself together with a tremendous effort.

"We must not stay here talking," he said. "Come with me. Leave your car; it will be seen to."

He snapped his fingers and one of the soldiers hovering in the background made a gesture towards another big limousine which was parked at the side of the airport buildings. It drove up and they all got into it. They all three sat in the back seat. A soldier sat in the front beside the driver and the two motor-bicyclists roared up to ride on either side of the car.

"Bing! What can I say to you?" the Moroccan asked in broken tones as they moved away.

"Don't say anything," Bing answered. "We had a bit of luck, that was all. I want to introduce you to Melina Lindsay who has been more wonderful than I can ever say. Her father was Sir Frederick Lindsay—you've heard me speak of him Mohammed?"

"But, of course," the Minister answered. "Sir Frederick Lindsay was a very great man."

He bent forward to take Melina's hand.

"How can I ever thank you for what you have done for me in saving my son?"

"It was Bing who did everything," Melina answered shyly.

The Minister unashamedly wiped the tears from his eyes.

"My wife and I had begun to believe it was hopeless," he said. "But she had more faith than I had, Bing. She made them hold the aeroplane even when the

193

officials said it was impossible and that they must move off according to schedule. She was sure you would come."

"We should have been here twenty minutes earlier if it had not been for Moulay Ibrahim's men at El-Guelb," Bing said. "They had a sort of ambush rigged up, but fortunately our friends in Marrakesh had telephoned to those who were loyal and they took us round the village over a camel track."

"They shall be rewarded," the Minister said. "If you will give me a list of everyone who has helped you, Bing, you can rely on my gratitude not only now but for ever."

"Thank you, Mohammed," Bing said. "I was certain you would say that."

"My boy! My little boy!" the Minister murmured. "If I had to give everything in the world I possess, it would not be enough."

"He is safe now, anyway," Bing said in a matter of fact voice as if such emotionalism was slightly embarrassing.

"He is safe enough for the moment," the Minister agreed "but who knows when Moulay Ibrahim will strike next?"

"Where are you taking us, by the way?" Bing inquired still in the cool, conversational tone which seemed to bring everything down to the ordinary and commonplace.

"To my house, of course," his friend replied. "I thought you would stay with me tonight. Tomorrow you must both leave the country. You will be a marked man, Bing, as you well know, and Miss Lindsay's life will also be in danger."

As he spoke the car drove into a big courtyard and they got out to step through a beautifully carved doorway into the cool, scented beauty of a house that was half Moorish and half French.

"What would you like to do first?" their host inquired.

"Personally," Bing replied, "I want a bath and some

decent clothes; and I expect Melina would like the same."

The Minister snapped his fingers. A maid appeared. She was a Frenchwoman and she led Melina upstairs to a magnificent bedroom with windows overlooking a flower-filled garden beyond which was a view of the sea.

"I think *Madame's* dresses will fit you, *Ma'mselle,*" she said looking at Melina appraisingly. "And His Excellency says that you are to choose anything that you desire."

"Thank you," Melina answered, beginning to pull the djellabah off and realising, as she did so, what a freak she looked with the kohl smudged round her eyes and the bridge of her nose red from where the yashmak had cut it.

It was unbelievable pleasure to sink into the hot, scented bath, and when she had soaked her tired limbs she washed her hair and saw again the dancing lights of gold and red as the thick dust was washed away.

She must have stayed in her bath for nearly an hour until she found her head nodding and she knew she was almost falling asleep. Self-preservation made her get out.

"I should look silly if I drowned myself now," she thought with a little smile as she rubbed herself dry in the big pale pink bath towel which matched the bathroom. She walked back into the bedroom to find that the bed was turned down invitingly and a light meal of eggs, fruit and milk was awaiting beside it on a tray.

"His Excellency has suggested that you should rest, *Ma'mselle,*" the maid explained. "He asked me to say that he and M'sieur Ward had things to discuss and it would be better for you to sleep a little and relieve your fatigue."

"I am tired," Melina admitted, thinking how little she had slept the night before and how early they had risen.

"Dinner is not until nine-thirty," the maid said, "but

in case *Ma'mselle* is hungry now the chef has made her a special omelette."

Melina ate a little of the omelette, drank the milk, and then almost as her head touched the pillow she was asleep.

She was awakened, it seemed to her to be hours later, by the sound of curtains being drawn and she felt a kind of radiant happiness because everything was all right. It was so different from the feeling of fear and apprehension which she had experienced at every other awakening recently. Now there was only happiness and the knowledge that in a very short time she would see Bing again.

She let the maid arrange her hair in a new and, Melina secretly thought, exceedingly becoming fashion. She allowed herself to be dressed in one of the gowns which hung in profusion in the wardrobe. It was a dress of pale blue chiffon embroidered with tiny diamante stars and it clung to her figure making her look very young and ethereal.

Melina could not help feeling glad that Bing would see her like this. She had never possessed a dress which had cost so much and she knew there was a special radiance about her as she ran downstairs to where she had been told Bing was waiting for her in the Salon.

He was not in the big room filled with flowers and exquisite gilt furniture and she stood for a moment, irresolute by the door, until she saw him sitting outside the big French windows which opened on to the garden. The Minister was with him and as Melina appeared they both rose to their feet.

"I hope my poor house has been able to provide you with everything that you needed," the Minister said ceremoniously as he raised her hand to his lips.

"Everything, thank you," Melina answered: but her eyes were on Bing, noting the sudden admiration in his face, feeling happier than she had ever done in her life before.

She settled down at the glass-covered table and accepted a glass of champagne brought to her by a servant in elaborate livery. From the same tray the Minister took a small glass of apricot juice for his religion forbade him alcohol. He rose to his feet and raised the glass in his right hand.

"To your health and to your happiness!" he said. "God bless you both!"

He drank and smiled at them benevolently.

"You must forgive me Miss Lindsay, if I leave you," he said. "I have an appointment this evening and it is very important that I should turn up apparently unconcerned by the events of the afternoon."

He glanced at them both for a moment and added with a twinkle in his eyes:

"I daresay you will not miss me so tremendously!"

Almost as soon as he was gone, dinner was served in a room also overlooking the garden, with the windows wide open and the tinkle of the fountain which was like music in their ears.

Afterwards Melina could never remember what she ate; she was too happy. She only knew that it was not the champagne but the excitement of being with Bing which made her feel as if everything they said was witty and enchanted. She could see his eyes looking at her; she could see the expression on his face, and that was more heady than any wine that she could have drunk.

When the meal was finished, they walked into the garden and sat amongst the roses and the honeysuckle with the fountain as the only sound to break the silence which came between them. Melina felt as if her voice was constricted in her throat before, at length, she managed to say:

"What time do we leave tomorrow?"

"You leave at eight-thirty," Bing answered. "The plane goes to Paris. You change there for London."

Melina felt as if a bomb had shattered something between them.

"But you . . . ! Aren't you . . . coming with me?"

She managed to stammer the words.

Bing shook his head.

"But, Bing!" she expostulated. "You . . . you must!

197

You heard what the Minister said. It is not safe for you to remain here."

"I know that," Bing answered, "but I have got to go back."

"But, why? Why?" she asked.

He turned round in the seat to face her. The sun was sinking somewhere out of sight, there was in the sky the glorious glowing colour which was intrinsically part of the East, but she saw the pain in his eyes.

"I love you, Melina!" he said quietly. "You know that, don't you?"

"I didn't think you . . . you cared for me?" she murmured.

"Oh, my sweet darling!"

He reached out and took her hands, crushing them between his until she could have cried out at the pain of it.

"I love you so completely, so absolutely," he said, "that I would never have believed I was capable of such emotion."

He paused for a moment and looked down at her hands and the marks he had made on them.

"Someone once said that love is dangerous," he said. "I believed that and I was determined never to fall in love again. I have been hurt once, damnably hurt. I wanted nothing to do with women—any of them."

He bent his head and kissed her fingers and she felt herself thrill to the touch of his lips.

"Then I met you," he went on. "I could hardly believe at first that you were as sweet as you are. I didn't know there was a woman in the world who would be so quick and intelligent, who could face danger without complaining and who would do what I asked her without argument."

He put his hand down as if he could not bear to touch her. His eyes were glowing as he looked into her face.

"I have been a brute to you in many ways," he continued. "I have told you nothing and made you obey me without question and without explanation. It

198

was because I could not credit you with being so absolutely marvellous, so utterly and completely all that a man could ask of a woman when they were in a desperate situation together."

"Oh, Bing, you make me so proud!" Melina whispered.

"That is what your father must be wherever he is at this moment," Bing replied. "Somehow I feel that he knows and is glad that he brought you up the way he did."

"He would have loved you too," Melina said.

Bing started at the sentence.

"Do you mean that you love me?" he said a little hesitantly, almost shyly.

"I have loved you for days—although it seems like years," Melina told him, the colour rising in her face. "I have loved you since that moment you kissed me when the searchlight was seeking us out on the hillside."

"I don't know what made me do it," he said, "except that already I was beginning to understand what you meant to me. I knew that I ought to send you away, that I shouldn't let you go on taking the risks that I was taking, gambling your life to help someone you had never met, someone of whom you had never even heard."

"If you had tried to send me away I shouldn't have gone," Melina retorted, and knew even as she said it that she would have had no choice in the matter.

"I ought to have left you with Rasmin in Fez," Bing said. "But I didn't for one reason, and one reason only—I wanted you to come with me."

"I am glad, so very glad," Melina whispered.

"I suppose love comes to everybody," Bing said. "They don't expect it; they fight against it; and suddenly it's there. You can't escape it. Melina, I love you! With all my heart and with all my soul."

Impulsively she put out her hands towards him, wanting him to take her in his arms, longing, with every nerve of her body, for the feel of his mouth

199

against hers. To her astonishment he ignored her gesture, turning his head sideways as if he could not bear to look at her.

"What is it, Bing?" she asked.

"I don't know how to tell you," he answered.

"What has happened? What has gone wrong?"

She heard the desperate tone in her own voice as she asked the question.

"I planned, as we were traveling to Marrakesh, during that exhausting journey in the bus, that if we came safely out of this, that if we survived in the pursuit of our enemies and got the child back to his parents, I would ask you to marry me."

"And aren't you ... going to do that?" Melina inquired.

"I somehow knew that you would look as you look tonight," Bing went on as if he had not heard her question.

"I imagined us together in a garden such as this. I told myself I would put my arms round you and say: 'You haven't known me very long, but I swear to you that I will make you a good husband and that if it lies within my power I will make you the happiest woman in the world'."

Bing's voice had died away and then suddenly he had pulled her into his arms and was holding her so tightly to him that she felt as if he crushed the very breath out of her body.

"I wanted to say that," he muttered in a kind of agony. "I wanted to say that—and now I can't."

"But, why ... why not?"

Melina looked up at him and realised that his mouth was very close to hers. Acting instinctively she put her arm round his neck and drew his head down to hers. She felt Bing's self control give as their lips met; felt the fiery passion of his kisses—on her mouth, her cheeks, her eyes and, finally, on the little pulse beating in her throat.

It was wild, delirious, crazy and she surrendered

200

herself utterly to the desire and emotion which seemed to have utterly swept him off his feet.

Then with a groan which seemed to come from the very depths of his being, Bing released her and, leaving her breathless and shaken on the seat, walked away across the garden to stand with his back to her, staring down into the fountain.

After a second she rose and walked after him.

"Please explain what is the matter, Bing," she said quietly.

"I'll try," he answered. "But for God's sake don't tempt me, don't drive me mad. Come out of this damned garden; I can't stand it."

He walked ahead of her into the Salon. The lights from the silken-shaded lamps glittered on the diamante on Melina's dress as she seated herself, white faced, on one of the needlework-covered sofas by the fireplace. Bing leant against the mantel-piece.

"If I touch you, I can't tell you what has happened," he said grimly. "So keep your distance."

Melina had held out her hand to him to draw him down beside her. Now it fell into her lap. She raised her puzzled, bewildered face towards his and waited.

"You know that we had no idea where the child was hidden in Marrakesh?" Bing said and his voice was harsh.

"Yes of course I knew that," Melina answered.

"We might never have found him," Bing said, "for Moulay Ibrahim had been extremely clever in his choice of a prison which no one would suspect as being one. Fortunately, one person—and one person only—could give me the information that I needed."

"Who ... was that?" Melina asked, and somehow she knew the answer even before Bing said it.

"Lileth!"

"Mrs. Schuster! But how should she know?"

"She motored down to Marrakesh with Moulay Ibrahim," Bing said. "I saw them arrive when I was standing outside the Moumania Hotel. Moulay Ibrahim had a good reason for inviting her to accompany him. He had seen her dancing with me—or one of his menials had reported that she had done so. He questioned Lileth closely about me, especially about my appearance. Only she could identify me for him. He knew she was indispensable to him."

"But, surely she must have guessed that he had a reason for questioning her?"

"She told me that she thought it was just idle curiosity," Bing said with a little twist of his lips.

"And in return he told her where the child was hidden?" Melina inquired incredulously.

"No, of course not," Bing answered. "But Lileth always had a retentive memory for detail—perhaps it was part of her training as a stenographer. Anyway, when I went to see her in the hotel she told me of everything that had transpired on their trip."

"You didn't tell me you were going to see her," Melina said with a flash of jealousy she could not prevent.

"I didn't know myself," Bing replied wearily. "I just saw her arrive in Moulay Ibrahim's car and I climbed up from the garden on to her balcony."

He paused for a moment as if remembering what had happened, before, with an obvious effort, he continued:

"Moulay Ibrahim had not suspected that Lileth would be interested in anything that he did or said. He knew that she had danced with me, but I don't think she told him that we had once . . . meant a great deal in each others' lives. Anyway, I don't think for one moment that he ever suspected we would get together again, as he knew I was on the run, hiding from him."

"But why did he tell her where the child was hidden?" Melina persisted.

"He didn't," Bing replied. "But outside the ramparts of Marrakesh the car was stopped by an Arab apparently begging for alms. Moulay Ibrahim searched in his pocket for a small coin to give him and as he handed it to him the Arab said in a voice which was meant to be a whisper: "Dar Al-Hamama!" As he spoke in Arabic

Moulay Ibrahim had never anticipated that Lileth, sitting beside him in the car, would understand Arabic."

"And does she?" Melina inquired. "She always told me she didn't speak any language except her own."

"That's true," Bing agreed. "But she knew one word of Arabic—the word *hamama*—because it means dove and it was an endearment I sometimes used to her."

His face flushed a little as he spoke and again Melina felt that stabbing dagger of jealousy turn over in her heart.

"It was just one of those long arms of coincidence which are always far more true in real life than in fiction," Bing said. "I was learning Arabic long ago in New York when we first knew each other, and I told her that one day I would build a house for her and call it Dar Al-Hamama—The House of the Dove."

He made a little gesture as he spoke as if he thrust aside those memories of the past.

"And when Lileth told me what the Arab had said I knew that Moulay Ibrahim, when he had hurried the child away from Fez, had not known exactly where the two men who escorted him would take their tiny prisoner. He must have had the choice of several houses in Marrakesh, but they had decided on Dar Al-Hamama and that was where he was."

Bing drew a deep breath before he continued:

"Once I knew exactly where I could find Suki it was imperative to extricate him before tomorrow, when his life was to be forfeit as an act of vengeance for the two traitors who will die at dawn."

There was silence, then Melina said:

"That isn't the end of the story, is it?"

"No," Bing answered. "Lileth asked her price for the information she was prepared to give me."

"Which was?" Melina's voice was hardly audible.

"That I should go back to her," Bing said.

"But you can't!" Melina cried jumping to her feet. "You can't do that, Bing! It's wrong! It's wicked! It's immoral! You don't love her, you love me. She can't make you go back in those circumstances."

203

She moved to him, her little hands reaching up to catch hold of the lapels of his coat, her head flung back, her eyes looking up into his.

He firmly loosened her fingers.

"I gave my word," he said, and his voice was dead and empty as if he had received the sentence of death.

"Let me go to her," Melina protested. "Let me plead with her. She can't understand that we love each other, that I belong to you . . ."

She stopped suddenly, her voice dying away on her lips. She knew how empty her words were. She knew that none of the things she was saying would count in the least with Lileth Schuster. She wanted Bing and she meant to have him.

"It's cruel!" Melina stormed. "It's cruel and wicked! Isn't there . . . anything we can do?"

"Nothing, my darling," Bing answered. "I love you and I know I will love you until my dying day. But I promised and so I shall go back. If Moulay Ibrahim kills me it won't matter very much, because without you I have no particular desire to go on living."

"Oh, Bing, perhaps something will happen. Perhaps she will grow tired of you. Perhaps she will see that you no longer love her and get bored. . . ."

As she spoke Melina knew it was no use. None of these things would happen. Lileth Schuster would hold on to Bing because she wanted him and nothing anyone could say or do would persuade her to let him go.

She shut her eyes, forcing herself to be silent, knowing that hysterical protests would only make it worse for Bing and could do no good.

"We are going to say good-bye now," she heard Bing say. "When you wake in the morning, I will not be here because I am going back to Marrakesh tonight."

"Please . . . don't! Please stay here with me," Melina wanted to say, but the words were choked in her throat. She wanted to offer herself to him; to tell him that she was his whether they were married or not. She belonged to him and that even if he must live with

204

another woman she would be his, both now and for eternity.

But her lips could not move and as if in some frightful, terrifying dream, she felt his arms go round her and knew it was for the last time.

He did not kiss her passionately as he had done before, but laid his cheek against hers and said, so softly that she could hardly hear it:

"Good-bye, my little love—my only love."

Just for a moment they clung to each other like children frightened in the dark, then Bing set Melina free and said in a voice deep and raw with agony:

"Go now! Go quickly while I can let you."

She turned obediently to obey him, too numb, too utterly devastated to say anything more, knowing only that in a few seconds the tempest of her tears rising within her would choke her voice and blind her from finding her way to the door.

Then, as she moved away from him, someone came into the room.

"M'sieur Ward," a voice said, "I have important news for you!"

They both looked at the newcomer. He was a young man whom Melina remembered seeing at the airport and who she guessed was an aide-de-camp to the Minister.

"What is it?" Bing asked.

"Moulay Ibrahim is dead."

"Dead!"

Bing ejaculated the word and for a moment Melina forgot her own sufferings in surprise at the announcement.

"How did he die?" Bing asked before the aide-de-camp could speak.

"As far as we can ascertain his car—which was travelling at well over a hundred kilometres an hour—had a burst tyre. It was caused, we believed, by a bullet."

"Where was this?" Bing asked quickly.

"Near the village of El Guelb."

Melina looked across the room at Bing. So Ahmed's cousin had helped them as he had promised.

"The car turned over several times and crashed down an embankment at the side of the road," the aide-de-camp went on. "The driver was flung clear. He is in hospital. Moulay Ibrahim, I understand, was killed instantly."

There was something like elation in his voice as he said the last words. He turned towards the door.

"I must go and find His Excellency and tell him the good news," he said with a smile on his face.

Then he paused.

"Oh, by the way, there was someone travelling with Moulay Ibrahim—an American lady. The police tell me from her passport that her name was Schuster—Mrs. Lileth Schuster. She was killed too."

The aide-de-camp went out of the room closing the door behind him. For a moment Melina and Bing stood staring at each other, then suddenly the space between them was no more and she was in his arms.

As he kissed her desperately as if they had both come back from the dead, the tears came running down her cheeks and she whispered over and over again:

"I love you! I love you! I love you!"